A
HODGEPODGE
OF
HORROR

BY TONY EVANS

First Edition © 2025 Tony Evans | Dark Holler Press
Cover design by: Kristina Osborn | Truborn Design
Book design by: A. A. Medina | Fabled Beast Design

Dark Holler Press #07
ISBN: 979-8-218-63181-9

www.tonyevanshorror.com

Follow me @tonyevanshorror

- For anyone who has given one of my books a chance -

From the bottom of my heart, thank you very much. You are

the reason I keep trying. I appreciate you.

"Where there is no imagination, there is no horror."

- Arthur Conan Doyle - A Study in Scarlet(Sherlock Holmes #1)

"Evil has only the power that we give it."

- Ray Bradbury – Something Wicked This Way Comes

TABLE OF CONTENTS

A BEDTIME STORY....................9

KATSARIDAPHOBIA....................21

THE DARE....................33

THE ANNUAL SOIREE....................47

THE DONKEY TREE....................57

BIG DADDY....................73

TROUBLE DOLLS....................89

A COLLECTION OF SOULS....................101

THE FINAL SACRIFICE....................117

MISS MOLLY, MISS MOLLY....................131

FECESNURA:
THE DEMON LORD OF SHIT....................155

ABOUT THE AUTHOR....................181

A BEDTIME STORY

"**P**lease, Daddy? Tell me a story. A really scary one this time." Billy's eyes were wide with excitement, a dog begging for his treat. "*Please*, Daddy? You've been gone for so long, and Mommy just can't tell scary stories like you can."

"Billy, I just got home. I'm tired. I'll read you one tomorrow, I promise. Okay?" He loosened his tie and tossed his bag to the corner. "Besides, you know Mommy doesn't like you hearing scary stories this late."

"But...Mommy's not here."

Billy's dad turned to him and sighed. "Yeah, well, I guess you have a point there."

"So..."

"Billy, I told you no. Where is she, anyway?"

"You mean Mommy? Oh...uhm...didn't you get her note?"

"Yeah, I saw it, but I could barely read it. She must've been in a hurry or something. The handwriting on the thing was absolutely horrible."

Billy's hand slid down the back of his head and scratched his neck. "Yeah...I guess she *did* seem like she was in a pretty big hurry. As soon as the storm started, she grabbed some soup and ran next door. She said something about Ms. Jones not feeling well. I think I heard her say *flu*."

"Oh, y...yeah. Uhm, sure, yeah," his father replied

nervously. "Ha! Ms. Jones, huh? Not bad," he mumbled quietly behind a grin before turning his full attention back to Billy. "She's always sick. I've never seen anybody have the flu as much as that woman. Well, either way, I wish she'd have waited. It's not safe to just run off and leave you here all by yourself. You never know what might happen."

"I guess," Billy replied innocently. "Well, you could tell me a story while she's gone. I know you could. You're a *great* storyteller, Daddy."

His father checked his watch and sighed as he shook his head. "Now Billy—"

A loud scratch across the window drew their attention, followed immediately by a flash of lightning that brightened the night sky to a daytime level. It startled Billy, causing him to jump. "Wh...what is that!" he screamed, throwing the covers over his head.

His father chuckled. "You see? Already scared, and nothing's even happened yet. It was just the branches from the tree outside. The wind blew them into your window. *This* is why Mommy doesn't want you to hear scary stories. Especially before bed. You'll be up for hours. Why don't you just go to sleep tonight? I really think it'd be better for everyone involved if you did."

"Daddy..." he whined, his lower lip pouting as it quivered. "It just startled me, that's all. I wasn't scared. I swear! Please? Tell me a story. I'll be brave. I promise I will."

His father stood in the doorway to the bedroom and stared, his outline nothing more than a dark silhouette against the lights of the hall. "Well, I don't know..."

"Please, please, *please*, Daddy?"

His father sighed and hung his head. "Why not? I guess I could, but just one, understand? Then it's straight to bed."

Excitement beamed from his eyes. "Oh boy! Just make sure it's a *really* scary one, okay?"

"I'll do my best, Billy."

§

His father closed the door until only a small crack remained. Through it, light from the hall slung a beam that broke the otherwise perfect darkness. Shadows cast across the bedroom floor appeared to be alive as they danced to the rhythm of the branches in the storm.

"Now, if you get scared in the middle of the night, you better not tell Mommy about any of this, got it? She'll already have my hide for telling you this. I'm not getting in trouble with her again."

"Okay, Daddy, I won't say a word, no matter *what*. But you don't have to worry. I won't be scared this time."

"We'll see about that," his father replied. "Get under the covers and I'll sit here in the chair next to you."

A sound came from downstairs just as a loud crash of thunder vibrated the house.

Billy flinched and looked at the door, then back to his father. "You mean you're not gonna sit in the bed with me, Daddy?"

"Nope, not tonight."

He looked around the room. The air was stale and motionless, giving Billy an eerie feeling that fell somewhere between loneliness and absolute isolation.

The sound came from downstairs again. This time, though, there was no thunder with it, and it sounded sort of like a dry rattle. No, a *clacking*. Yeah…it sounded like something clacking together.

Billy jerked his head toward the door. "Well, I'm not scared, Daddy. I just wanted to be able to grab you. You know, just in case…in case something were to happen."

The sound again. Rattling, clacking.

"You don't think Mommy's back, do you? That noise could have been her opening the door."

"It's just the ice maker in the refrigerator, Billy. Nothing to be afraid of." He pulled the desk chair over to the bedside and plopped down. "Now, let's see. What story should I…ah! I know!" He leaned back and stared at Billy; a crazed look covered his face. "Have I ever told you about *Bloody Bones*?"

Billy bit down on his lower lip and pulled the blankets up to his neck. "Bloody Bones? No, not that I can remember. I've never heard of him. Sounds kinda creepy."

"Creepy? More like downright horrifying," his father replied, clearing his throat and lowering the tone of his voice. "Now, I've never seen him, but your grandpa used to tell us about him all the time."

"Really?"

"Yep. He's kinda like the boogeyman around these parts, only scarier." He relaxed his body and unbuttoned the collar of his shirt. "Based on the name, Bloody Bones, I guess you can gather what he looks like?"

"Well, yeah, I think so, anyway. I guess he has bloody bones?"

"Oh yeah," his father laughed. "And he leaves a bright red trail of blood wherever he goes."

His mind a thousand miles away, Billy stared into

the darkness. His imagination conjured images of bloody skeletons roaming the streets of his neighborhood, leaving behind a crimson trail for all to follow.

"A blood trail, huh? Why does he do that, Daddy?"

"Because he has no skin. His bones are held together by long, thin strips of muscle. His veins and arteries weave throughout the tissue, holding everything in place. And the *blood*. So much *blood*, Billy."

Billy swallowed hard. "And he drips it everywhere? The blood I mean?"

"You see, Bloody Bones wants his skin back, and he wants it *real* bad."

"This *is* a scary story, Dadd—"

"Some people around here say he was burned alive; that the skin just melted off his body. Others say he was skinned and field dressed like a deer or rabbit. Nobody really knows, though. Personally, I think he was skinned. If he'd burned, his muscles would be melted and he wouldn't be able to move, right?"

Billy nodded nervously.

"But he moves, Billy. He moves very well. In fact, he roams around this sleepy little town every single night just after sunset, looking for unsuspecting victims."

Billy's eyes grew wide. He took a deep breath. "Unsuspecting victims? Victims...for what?"

"Ha! What do you think?"

"Oh," Billy said, anxiety filling his voice. "Skin?"

"Exactly. *Skin.*"

Billy began to shake. "How does he get it, Daddy? The skin, I mean."

"Now that's a good question." He straightened up in the chair and grinned. "He takes it from the bones of the child's parents, methodically though, so it all stays in one piece. He uses his long, pointy claws to make a slit down their backside, and he just peels it off like a glove."

"And what does he do with it, then?"

"He slips it over his body and wears it like a sweater."

Billy gasped.

"Only problem is, it never fits." He loosened the watch on his wrist and shrugged his shoulders, adjusting himself to be more comfortable. "So, he just keeps trying. Maybe that's why Mommy isn't back yet. Maybe ol' Bloody Bones is over there right now wearing *her* skin."

"Stop it, Daddy! You're *trying* to scare me!"

"Scare you?"

"That's not real! None of that is real! If he keeps trying to get a skin that fits, how come nobody ever goes missing, huh? Tell me that, Daddy!"

"Well, Billy, that's because he hasn't needed one for quite some time. You see, back when I was a little boy, a group of grown-ups got together and offered Bloody Bones a sacrifice. One perfect skin for thirty years of peace."

"Oooohhhh."

"One skin and one good meal, actually. I haven't even told you what he does to little kids, yet."

In a long, drawn-out whisper, Billy responded, "liiitttttllllle kiiiiddddds? Wh...what, Daddy?"

His father lowered his head, his voice taking an even deeper tone. "Why, he eats them, Billy. Gobbles them right down."

"Why does he do that?"

"It starts with a scratching noise at the door. You'll hear a faint whisper. '*Bloody Bones is at the door*', he'll say. You'll hear the clack of his feet across the wooden floor, every step louder than the last as he gets closer and closer. The sound of his finger scratching against the wall will be next, and it'll be smearing blood wherever it travels. '*Bloody Bones is in the living room*', he'll say. Thump, thump, thump, as his bare and bony feet thud on the carpet of the stairs, the sound of blood squishing with every step he takes."

"Daddy, when's Mommy coming home? I don't think I like this—"

His father pounded his feet on the floor to mimic the sound of footsteps. "'*Bloody Bones is on the stairs*', he'll call."

"Daddy, you're...you're scaring me." He was frozen, a rigid statue of flesh.

Coming within inches of Billy's face, his father leaned over and whispered. "You'll hear his bony fingers clawing at your door as he scratches at the handle, trying to get it." He clacked his fingernails against the wooden bed frame. "Out of nowhere, '*Bloody Bones is in your room, Billy*', he'll say."

A heavy wind whistled around the corner of the house, blowing branches and heavy rain into the window again.

"Yikes," Billy yelled, pulling the covers over his head.

His father laughed and stood up. "Okay. That's enough. Time to go to bed now. You wanted a scary story, and you got one." He scooted the chair back to the desk and checked his watch nervously. "Where *is* your mother?"

"Why, we're right here," a feminine voice said from behind.

Billy jerked the covers away from his head. "Mommy!

You're home!"

"It's about time," his father said, suddenly and obviously annoyed. "I wasn't sure you'd actually go through with it. For fuck's sake, I was starting to get worried."

Confused, Billy looked at his mother and father. "What are you talking about? Go through with what?"

"Shut up, Billy!" his father yelled. "Don't make this any harder than it has to be."

"What are you talking about?" Billy whined.

"Billy, you know that story I just told you? Bloody Bones? Well, it was kinda true."

Billy scooted away, his back against the wall as he cuddled his blankets.

"And those thirty years of peace I mentioned for that sacrifice? Well, it's up tonight."

Billy's eyes were wide, and he began to tremble. "I don't understand."

"Let's just say Mommy and I made a little deal with Bloody Bones to extend this peace. We can't afford to have him starting back up around here. Too many kids go missing. You understand? Kinda the whole, sacrifice one to save a thousand mentality." He looked at his wife. "So, did Ms. Jones come to help or what? I don't wanna hurt him too bad before Bloody Bones gets here," he glanced back at Billy, "and you know *he's* not gonna go easy."

"Yeah, she came," Billy's mother said. "Not sure how much help she'll be, though. She actually does seem pretty sick. She's moving like a damn zombie. I don't know what's wrong with her."

"That damn woman. It's all in her hea—"

Billy started laughing. It was quiet at first, barely even noticeable. Then it grew louder and louder, drowning out the sound of the now raging storm.

His mother and father stared at him, uncertain that he actually understood his impending fate.

"What are you laughing at? You *do* understand what's about to happen, don't you?"

Billy continued to laugh uncontrollably. The sound of dull thumps echoed in the hall as Ms. Jones stumbled into the doorway. Eyes sunk into their sockets, her skin hung loose and floppy as a small dribble of spit slid down her chin.

"*Jesus*," Billy's father blurted out. "What's *wrong* with you?"

"Rhonda? Are you okay?" Billy's mother asked.

"She's fine, guys," Billy said. "In fact, everything's absolutely *perfect*."

His parents turned to him as he spoke.

"You see, I overheard you two talking about a week ago. I heard you planning the whole thing. How you were gonna serve me up to Bloody Bones so he would leave for another thirty years?"

Billy tried to hold it back, but his laughs had to come out. He slapped the bed hard with each hilarious outburst, laughing as only a deranged psychopath or child does.

"Bloody Bones came to visit a couple nights ago, but you guys were already asleep. He scared me at first, but he said he couldn't take me until tonight, right when the thirty years was up. Then, he explained what he *really* wanted, one good skin and two good meals. So, *we* made a deal."

From behind, a loud slurping sound sent a chill into their

bones. Billy's mother and father turned to see Ms. Jones; her face replaced by a blood coated patchwork of exposed muscle stretched over bone. In her left hand, a flesh-colored sack covered in long, curly, brown hair hung loose; a dark crimson liquid dripping to her feet.

A scream filled the room as Billy's mother fell back, crashing to the floor. His father turned to him, fear taking over. "Wh-what have you done, Billy? Y-you don't know what you're doing!"

"You forgot the best part of the story, Daddy. My favorite part, actually. What is it that Bloody Bones says? You know, right before he gets the skin from the parents?"

"Take them! Take her!" He yelled, pointing to his wife as she clawed toward the wall, trying to stand. In a frantic attempt to escape, his father made a leap for the door as he tried to push past the creature.

With one hand, Bloody Bones gripped his father's throat and held him above the floor as he kicked and flailed trying to free himself, gurgles and grunts the only sounds made.

"Oh, yeah. I remember now," Billy said with a grin. "He says, 'Bloody Bones has got you!'"

KATSARIDAPHOBIA

JIM TURNED THE KNOB AS FAR TOWARD THE RED LINE AS IT would go. The water had to be hot. That's the only way it would kill them. The doctors said it would help him; they'd said it would ease his nervousness, his fears.

"Goddamn bugs." He looked into the drain; eyes focused. An intense stare. The sound of water swirling down into the darkness helped to comfort him, at least a little. A steady and uninterrupted flow meant nothing was waiting to surprise him.

A hand found his lower back, massaged it gently. "Calm down, honey," Janie said in a soothing voice. "You know there's nothing there." She slid her hand up and rested it on his shoulder.

"You think it, don't you, Janie? You really think I'm crazy."

"No, Jim. I *know* you're not. The doctors, they said you were cured, remember? It's a sickness. I've looked it up." Her eyes were wide, a sympathetic smile on her lips. "I'm sorry. I just wanted to—"

"Yeah, I know," he interrupted. "You just wanted to remind me of how crazy I am. Jim, your husband, the nut job." He turned to Janie; his head hung low. "It is, you know. Crazy."

"No, it's not, and neither are you, Jim. It's a disease. No different from being afraid of spiders or small spaces. What's it called again?"

He shook his head and snorted. "Katsaridaphobia," he

said, grimacing. "What a nasty, stupid word. A grown man, afraid of *cockroaches*." A chill crept up his legs, running through his spine before tightening around his stomach. Just mentioning that word forced him to gag.

"That was thirty years ago. Try to forget about it, okay? They're...well, they're not real. They explained that to you. Remember?"

"Yeah, sure. I remember," he said, shaking his head. "They may not be real, but the memories are." His brows scrunched, concern and anxiousness covered his face. "You weren't there. You didn't have to see it, to *feel* it. *You* didn't feel their legs gripping the hair on *your* arms, antennae probing *your* nostrils, the fluttering sound their disgusting little wings made as they descended from every dark corner of that house, covering *you* like a goddamn living blanket." He shuddered and turned toward his wife, hugging her. "You know, I was fine. I'd pushed it out of my mind, forgotten about it, almost. Then I saw one at work. Fucking disgusting little goddamn nasty cockroaches."

"I know. You'll get through it, Jim. *We'll* get through it. Together. Do you hear me?"

She stepped back and gestured toward the shower. A dense fog covered the mirror, the air thick and heavy with steam. "You think it's been long enough?"

"Considering it's all just my imagination and nothing's in there anyway, I'd say yes." He chuckled, then sighed deeply. "Thanks, Janie. I really appreciate your putting up with my craziness. You're a good wife."

§

Water pelted his back, and the heat stung at first before he acclimated. It felt good to him now. It helped relax him, take his mind away from those goddamn bugs.

His hands against the wall, he concentrated on the sound of water rushing over his body and crashing into the tub. Its rhythm consistent, only changing if he moved from one side to the other. He smiled, rocked back and forth, dancing with the beat of the sounds.

Then it happened.

His eyes sprung abruptly open, and he came to a complete stop. At first, he thought it was just the water. But the second time, the third, that's what made him really take notice.

This sound wasn't one of liquid bouncing off of a hard surface. This sound was different.

It wasn't the characteristic *thud* or *splat* the other droplets were making, of that, he was quite sure. It was still strangely familiar, though, and he knew he'd heard it before.

It sounded more like a *flutter*.

Jim's heart accelerated while his breathing became shallow and rapid.

He closed his eyes. It was happening again. Another episode, as his doctors had called them.

"Wings. That sounds like...wings," he whispered. "It fucking sounds like *wings*." He remembered what the doctors had told him to do in situations like this when he started to *imagine* them. He began to repeat the mantra.

"They're not real. They're not real."

He opened the shower curtain just enough to see and peered out, as if spying on a nosy neighbor from a bedroom window. He scanned the room carefully before coming to a sudden stop.

In the corner, on the wall just below the air vent, he saw it. It scurried around the edge of the vent cover, its light brown body a perfect contrast with the shell-white walls. It taunted him, fluttering from wall to wall, back and forth like some sort of old sadistic friend.

"No. It's...it's not real. It can't be." He squinted tightly and repeated the phrase.

"They're not real, they're not real, they're not real."

Slowly, he opened his eyes. "God...no," he said, gasping.

Still in the same spot, the bug stared at him, waving its little legs as if speaking to him, gesturing to him to come forward, to say hello.

Hey there, Jim. How's it goin'? Remember me? I've missed you, Jimbo!

"Janie! Janie, get in here, now!" He focused on the bug intently, keeping it in his sights. He had to keep an eye on it to make sure Janie could see it, to make sure he wasn't just losing his mind.

The door flung open. "What is it, Jim?"

"There, do you see it?"

"Are you oka—"

"Look, Janie!" he yelled, pointing to the corner. "Do you see it or not?"

Confused, she looked to where he was pointing. "See what, Jim?"

"Look, goddamn it!" he shouted. "It's right there!"

"What is it? I don't see anything."

"What do you mean, you don't see anything?" He looked at his wife and back to the corner. "It's right—" A sickening chill engulfed his entire body. The roach was gone. Jim looked at the vent, then at Janie. "I don't understand. It must have—"

"Are you okay?" Janie asked, sympathetically. "You did take your medicine?"

He looked at the floor, his lips tightening in embarrassment. "I'm good. Yes. I took it. Sorry to have bothered you." He pulled the curtain enough to stop the spray of the shower from hitting the floor. "I've gotten everything all wet. I'm sorry. I'll clean it up when I'm finished."

"Jim?"

"I'm okay. I promise. But I'm not crazy, Janie."

"Please, honey. I—"

He pulled the curtain closed. "I'm not crazy, Janie. I just thought I saw something. I was wrong. It happens, you know."

"Are you sure?"

"I told you I'm fine," he said sternly.

"Jim, I just—"

"Leave me alone, Janie, please? I'll be finished in a bit."

§

Jim wet his hair and wiped the water back over his head before moving the curtain to look at the corner again.

"Maybe I did imagine it." He stared at the space as he grew uncertain of himself. "But I saw it. Or, at least, I *think* I did. Goddamn nasty bugs. Gonna be the death of me one way or another."

He opened the shampoo bottle and turned it upside down. "I *know* it was there, though. It *had* to be real. I even *heard* the goddamn thing." The gel covered his hand, spilling into the tub. He placed the bottle to the side and thought of other possible explanations, those that didn't include him being crazy but still somehow explained the absence of any real bug.

"Forget it, Jim. It wasn't real," he told himself.

He massaged the shampoo into his hair as his hands worked around the sides and back of his head. The excess soap dripped down onto his shoulders and neck, tickling him. As his hand slid down to wipe it away, he felt a hard mass on his skin.

Goosepimples covered his arms, forcing his shoulders to hunch up in a defensive posture. "What the fuck!" he shouted.

He grasped at the thing, pulling something large and squishy away. Without thinking, he flung it toward the wall as a hefty grunt forced from his lungs. The object bounced off the wall and onto the shower floor, landing on its back.

"You've gotta be fuckin' kiddin' me!"

At his feet lay a large cockroach, at least two inches in length. Its body was a light brown in color, its legs wiggling as it tried to regain position.

Jim staggered back. "You can't be real." Eyes squeezed shut, he repeated the mantra, screaming it now. "You're not real, you're not real, you're not real!"

He opened his eyes. The insect was there, fighting the flow of the current like a salmon desperately trying to swim upstream.

Again.

"You're not real, you're not real, you're not real!"

He paused; it was the moment of truth.

Jim's eyes opened. In place of the one roach was ten, fifty, a hundred, emerging from the shower drain like angry bees from their hive.

"Wha...what the hell!"

He jumped back, slamming against the wall. He felt

something squirm up his leg and looked down to see. Cockroaches - squeezing from every crack, every crevice. They came up from the grout in the tile, from the shower head, the drain. They emerged in droves, their numbers too great to count.

Jim flailed, fighting for something to hold as his feet slid from under him. He grasped the curtain, but his weight was too much for the flimsy rod to hold. As he crashed to the floor, his head slammed against the vanity; its contents spilling on top of him.

Roaches spread over every square inch of his skin, filing in like little soldiers marching to their leader's orders. He slapped at them, but it did no good. There were just too many.

His screams echoed in the small room as sharp mandibles pierced his skin, ripping small chunks of flesh away from the bone with each and every bite. Tiny droplets of blood dribbled onto the floor, outlining his body against the white tile.

"You're not real!" he cried, trying to convince himself it was all in his imagination.

He glanced toward the closet door just as something large squeezed from beneath. The cockroach was the size of a small dog, flattened out to fit through the tiny crack. Jim couldn't believe his eyes.

It was a huge cockroach.

A *king* cockroach.

It climbed onto the toilet to watch its subjects as they worked to dismantle Jim. "Stop his screaming," the king ordered in a burly voice.

Hordes of cockroaches filled his throat, his lungs. With his airway blocked, he could no longer scream. He was forced to watch in silence.

"Do you remember us, Jim?"

His mouth was wide, but there was no sound escaping.

"Why did you let them take us away? We've missed you." It cocked its head as if studying Jim, watching as he clawed at his throat for oxygen. "No worries, though. We've come to take you home. We've come to take you back to Hell with us." Like a general commanding his troops, the king whipped his long, thread-like antennae. "Continue."

The roaches chewed their way through his skin, burrowing deep into the tissue.

Jim ripped at his arms and legs, but the pain was becoming unbearable. As he flailed about, he noticed his razor beside him on the floor; it had fallen when he broke the vanity. Suddenly, a thought came to him.

I'll cut them out!

He scrambled to his knees, and as he did, the feeling of insects exploding under his weight, squishing under his skin from the force between bone and tile. He began to cut, slicing through meat and muscle. With each swipe, the roaches dug deeper until they were clinging to solid bone. He cut everywhere. His face, stomach, arms. Blood leaked from every wound, pooling on the tile floor around him like shallow scarlet mud puddles. Each time he cut into himself, he ripped handfuls of giant cockroaches from his body, crushing them with his fist.

"Jim! Are you okay?" a voice yelled from the other side of the door. "What's going on in there?"

"They're everywhere, Janie!" he screamed. "They're fucking everywhere!"

She grabbed the handle and pushed to open the door, but it wouldn't budge. "Jim, it's locked! It won't open!"

"They're eating me alive!"

She moved back, placing as much space as possible between herself and the door. With a force unlike any she'd ever drawn on, she thrust herself into the door shoulder first, breaking it free. She fell to the ground as it burst open, and in front of her, slicing away at his own skin, lay Jim.

"Run, Janie! Run!" he screamed.

For the first time, she could see them. For the first time since this had all started, she *knew* without any doubt that her husband wasn't crazy, that it wasn't all just in his mind. The roaches covered him from head to toe, and they were chewing on his skin like little bits of jerky.

"Jesus, Jim!"

From the toilet seat, the king roach commanded, "attack her! She cannot live!"

In an instant, they flocked toward her, running from Jim's mouth and throat, finally giving him enough room to breathe. She scrambled to her feet and kicked the first wave hard, sending them crashing against the walls.

"This can't be real!" she yelled in terror.

As Jim clambered around on the floor, slipping in his own blood, Janie watched the king beast rise up to his hind legs like a bear. "You will both die here today!" he screamed, swinging his four unused limbs, wildly.

"Jim, I'm going to get you out of here," Janie yelled. In a moment of bravery, determined to save her husband, she fought over and around the sea of insects, stomping and kicking them as she went. "You can't have him!" she screamed.

"He's not yours!" She saw a small glint of brightness reflected from the floor, a bit of glass from the shattered mirror. "It's time to get rid of you, once and for all!" She reached down and took a long shard of jagged glass into her hand, her blood mixing with that of Jim and the bugs.

They began to cover her, bite her, ripping into her flesh effortlessly. The king laughed, a boisterous sound that echoed against the hard surfaces of the room. "You have no chance. We *always* win!" He yelled, stroking his long antennae with his forelegs.

"Not this time!" Janie flung a handful of the roaches from her face, and in one hard swipe, the rough edge of the broken mirror sliced into the sternum of the giant king.

"No!" he cried, as a thick, greenish substance oozed from the wound. Like a loose brick falling to the earth, his lifeless body made a dull thud against the floor of the bathroom. Immediately, the crowd of insects began to melt away, their juices mixing into the bloody concoction that covered everything in sight.

Blood oozed from countless gashes and cuts covering Jim's skin. "Janie! Are you...are you okay?"

She took a towel from the wrack and wiped her arms, then tossed it to Jim. Her eyes were wide, a look of disbelief mixed with triumph covered her face. "It's over, Jim. It's finally over. I told you we'd get through this together, didn't I?"

THE DARE

"**T**HIS IS IT? THIS IS HOW YOU AIM TO SCARE ME?" Tim stood at the end of the long driveway looking back at the trees as they arched over its entire length, shielding it from any remaining vestiges of sunlight the late October evening had to offer. One eyebrow cocked, he turned and faced Gina with a look of arrogance that only a teenage boy is capable of. She was, after all, the girl who'd thought it wise to bet against the new kid, to *dare* him he wouldn't do something so simple. The one thing she didn't think to take into account, though, was that when you're a new kid in a new town...you *have* to look arrogant and cocky, and you *can't* turn down such an easy dare.

"Yeah. This is it, all right. The Baily House."

The two of them glanced up at the structure, a combination of bad lighting from the setting sun mixed with a chilled autumn breeze playing a dangerous game with the shadows around its gables. The way they moved, flittering about on the edges of the walls, the silhouettes of leafless limbs dancing around with each gust, all of it gave the impression that the surrounding forest, the house itself, even, was alive.

Tim grinned, tilted his head to the side. "Oh, I get it. This is supposed to be a haunted house. That's it, right?" He nodded, ran one hand through his hair. "Look, I don't know what kind of stories you guys have around here, folktales or legends or whatever, or what you *normally* do to haze the new kids on the block, which I obviously am, but I can guarantee you one thing..." He paused for a moment; his eyes wide with confidence as he gauged Gina's reaction. Her attention was still on him, so that was a good thing, at least. "If this is the best you've got, you might as well just give up now and concede defeat, because this..." he gestured toward the house, "just ain't gonna cut it. I mean, come on. Aren't we a little old to be afraid of haunted houses and ghosts? I don't even believe in those things, girl."

"Well," Gina said, a wry smile stretching across her pouty lips, growing larger as she thought through her words carefully before speaking. "First off, I never said I was trying to scare you. All I said was that most people around here are too scared to go inside. I don't care if you're scared of this place or not." She took a step closer to him, one hand fiddling with her thick, auburn curls, the other stuffed in her hip pocket. "And neither does she."

Tim could feel his heart rate increase as Gina closed the distance between them, the slow, steady thump in his chest becoming more frantic and fast paced as a myriad of hormones dumped into his bloodstream. She was very pretty, after all, and he wasn't used to such pretty girls giving him the time of day. This, he both realized, and was extremely grateful for in this moment, was one of the few good things about changing towns and schools as a teenager. It was like a fresh start, as stupid as he knew that sounded. Nobody knows you, and most people show an interest, for one reason or another, at least initially.

"She?" He looked around at the other kids standing idly

behind Gina, trying to see if this *She* that had been spoken of was present. From the expressions on their faces, those Tim had chalked up to stupid fear and nervousness, he could tell that wasn't the case. These kids were nothing more than the few in town who weren't too scared to come along and see if he would really carry through with it.

"Yes. *She*."

He waited for Gina to continue, to elaborate a bit more on this subject, but she never did. Instead, she just continued with her initial thought.

"And secondly," Gina continued, "the deal, if I recall, was that I'd go out on a date with you...*if*... you survive a walk-through of this house. Gotta go in, check out *all* the rooms, and come back out."

She took another step toward him; they were almost face to face now. He could smell the sweet scent of vanilla around her, a scent that instantly pulled him in and took his mind to much better places.

"Well," she said, looking up at Tim as she lightly bit her lower lip. "What do you say, new kid? You think you can handle that minor little task?"

Tim chuckled nervously, his confident demeanor starting to wane. Not because of the house or the dare. No, not at all. He wasn't worried about any of that. It was just a house, and nothing more. The only difference in this one and any other he'd ever set foot in being that this one was vacant, or at least it *appeared* to be. None of this bothered him at all.

The other kids staring at him, though, that made him slightly uncomfortable. Just standing there like a bunch of robots or mannequins, their eyes fixed on his every move.

What were they doing? Why were they even there? Were they just a bunch of losers from around town that didn't have anything better to do? A bunch of rejects that hoped to watch him make a fool of himself?

And then there was Gina. She was definitely making him nervous, but in a different way. In a good way. She made his blood hot, made his stomach shaky and swirly and weak. She made his heart race. She excited him, and he loved that feeling.

"What do *I* say? Am *I* up to the task?" He looked to the other kids again. All of them just standing there, motionless, mouths hanging open like a bunch of braindead zombie freaks. Tim shook his head, their rudeness sickening, the thought of how scared they seemed to be of this house so foreign to him that he couldn't even comprehend it. "I say, hell yes, I'm up to it! Let's go!"

Gina's mouth opened slightly, her tongue sliding between ruby lips, moistening them, an act that sent Tim's heart into overdrive. "You're sure, then? You're sure you wanna go inside?"

"I said yeah, didn't I? What more do you want?"

"I'm just making sure, because once you say it...once you step inside...there's no goin' back. That's just how it works here, got it?"

"Huh? What do you mean, that's just how it works? I'm not sure I follow."

Gina smiled. She licked her lips again, leaned in closer. "I just wanna make sure you're up for it. That's all. I mean...you certainly...*look* like the kind of boy that can handle himself, no matter the situation. That sound about right?"

He squinted his eyes as if studying her, the way she moved,

the small little subtleties in her expressions driving him wild, and suddenly whatever it was she'd just said was forgotten. He thought about the consequences of what was about to happen, those of their agreement. If he could pull this off, and surely to God he could – after all, what's to walking through a vacant house? – then she'd most certainly be the prettiest, most attractive girl that'd ever paid him any mind.

I got this, he thought. *Piece of fuckin' cake.*

"If it means going out on a date with you, absolutely. This'll be no problem. I'll go in and show you, girl. This place ain't nothin'."

"Let the record show," she said to the others, "he's agreed to go inside."

The others whispered to themselves, their dull and emotionless expressions changing to expressions of genuine interest.

Tim chuckled, slightly surprised. "What is this? Am I on trial or something? Let the record show? What's all that about?"

One side of her mouth curled up just a bit more than the other, and Gina placed one hand on Tim's cheek. "Oh, it's nothing, really. Just something we do. You've got this, remember? Piece of cake," she said, turning to grab a flashlight from her backpack. "I'm guessing you don't have one, since I don't see a pack or anything on you?"

Tim was silent for a moment as his mind tried to make sense of what was happening. 'Let the record show' and 'that's just how it works here'? What was that about? He certainly wasn't afraid of a so-called haunted house, but something definitely didn't seem right about this one, about this situation. They were acting strange, regardless of his beliefs on the afterlife.

"Well?"

"Oh...uh, a flashlight. No. I don't have one."

"Didn't think so." She walked over to the other kids and said something to them in a low voice.

"Hey," Tim started. "What are you guys talkin' abo—"

"Well," Gina said, turning back toward him. "Are you ready?"

"Oh, uh...well...sure. I guess. You're coming too?"

"Well, yeah. How else will we have proof, silly?"

Tim grinned. "Proof? Proof of what?"

"Proof that you went in, of course."

"I mean...I'll be right back out."

"Oh, yeah. Right. Well, this is sort of a tradition we have, the way we do things around here. You understand, I'm sure. And we don't much like breaking tradition."

Out of nowhere, the gears clicked in his mind like a well-oiled machine. *Proof! Of course! There's someone in there waiting to scare me. That's why she's going in. She's gonna make sure they find me and probably video it all. It makes perfect sense!*

"You about ready," Gina said, interrupting Tim's thoughts.

Tim smiled and nodded slowly. "Absolutely. Bring it on."

She gestured toward the rusty iron rod fence at the end of the drive that separated them from the house. "After you."

§

"So," Tim said, stopping to place his foot on the first step up to the porch. "Do you do this to all the guys that aren't from these parts?" He turned back to Gina, who was following immediately behind him, and grinned.

"Do what? Bring them out here? Or do you mean let them take me on dates if they survive?"

Tim cocked an eyebrow, amused at her response. "Either, or, I guess?" Grabbing the handrail, he shifted his weight forward onto the first step. "Is that an admission that you *do* bring lots of guys out here?"

Gina laughed, her sarcasm on point. "Oh, absolutely. The problem is, though, that none of them have taken me out yet, because none of them have ever made it out of the house."

"Oh? You must be a regular little black widow."

Gina's jaw dropped. "Well, now...a sharp tongue *and* a sense of humor, huh? You really *are* something special, aren't you?" She slapped him on the arm playfully.

"Yeah, that's what they tell me. And by *they*, I mean my momma. She tells me that all the time." He faced the house again and started toward the door. The steps creaked and groaned under his weight as he pushed on to the second, then the third, and for a moment, he wasn't sure whether the old wood had enough strength left to hold their weight.

As they made it up onto the porch, the first thing he noticed were the windows. There were two of them, one on either side of the door, each covered in a thick, milky-white film from what had to be years neglect. Tim reached out and wiped at one with the cuff of his shirt sleeve, but it was no use. The substance had long since dried and become a permanent fixture on the glass.

"Jesus, this place is a mess. What's the story here?"

"Story? What do you mean?"

"Every haunted house has a story. This place is supposed

to be haunted, so what's the story? What is it, people were murdered here? It used to be a funeral home? Name any other typical haunted house trope and insert here." He walked over, placed his hand on the doorknob, and gave it a jiggle. To his surprise, there was no resistance. "I guess we just go on in, then?" he asked, pushing the door open.

He gave the door a push and the pungent smell of rotting wood and mildew passed over them as a rush of stale air was forced from the house. Tim raised his arm to cover his face, and the dust riding on the breeze made him cough.

"Holy shit," he said, waving his arms back and forth as he tried to waft the mold ridden allergens away from his nostrils. "And I thought the *outside* was bad!"

"Yeah, I could've told you it wasn't much better in here," Gina replied. "I figured you'd have enough sense to figure that one out. The whole house is in pretty bad shape."

"Got jokes, huh?"

"I'm just sayin', it's in pretty bad shape. And, as far as the story goes, this really isn't your *typical* haunted house. You see, there wasn't anything horrible done here, no bad deeds or old funeral homes, and it wasn't built on top of some sacred burial ground or anything."

Tim stepped inside, careful not to trip on any unseen objects in the dark. "Really? Doesn't sound like anything too scary or haunted to me, then. What makes it so special? I mean, if nobody died here, or there wasn't some horrible act committed or something like that, why's it haunted?"

"Here," Gina said, turning on her flashlight and handing it to him. "You'll need this more than me."

He took the flashlight and shined it around the room. "It's

dirty as hell, that's for sure, but other than that, it doesn't look too scary."

"Right. *This* room isn't, at least."

Tim paused for a moment, turned back to face Gina. "This room? Oh, I see. So, there's only one room that's haunted? Is that the deal here? Was somebody tortured there? An old woman left to die or something?" He turned around and continued inspecting the room, walking toward the staircase. As he aimed the light's beam up and down the steps, something caught his attention. "Are those...footprints?" He knelt down to get a closer look.

"Something like that," Gina said. "The spirit, if you want to call her that, is sort of confined to one place. She likes it there, feels at home there, you could say."

Tim was halfway up the stairs now, stopping on every step to take a closer look. "Are you seeing this, or am I going crazy? These are footprints, right?" He placed his own foot over one of the prints, matching it almost flawlessly. "Nobody lives here, do they? Maybe there's some homeless person hanging around."

Gina laughed. "There are no homeless people staying here. They wouldn't last a night. She's very hungry. Always hungry."

His attention fully on finding out where the footprints went, Tim wasn't really processing what was being said. "But...these *are* footprints. They have to be, right?" He looked at them, a trail leading from the front door to at least the top of the stairs. Footprints, impressions pressed into a thick layer of dust that covered the rest of the floor. "That has to be what they are, but who do they belong to?" As he reached the top of the staircase, he saw that they continued down the hall, stopping in front of a door at the end of the long, dark corridor. "It looks like they go to a room up here. I bet there's someone staying in there," he said, walking down the hall slowly toward the door.

"It wasn't original to the house. That room, I mean. It was an add on. According to the story, the wood used to build it came from an old oak that used to set at the top of the hill out back. They say that that particular tree was used as a hanging tree, and unfortunately, it was used to hang her. They said she was a witch, you see? But she wasn't. That didn't stop her from calling on Satan right before she dropped to her death on that tree, though. She cursed the town and swore her revenge, and they say that Satan gave her powers. Only thing is, she's tied to that tree, which is now in the walls of this room. He gave her powers, though. Strong ones. Powers over this town, ways to keep us under her thumb, her control. But she's not a person anymore. She's a spirit...a dark one. Like I said, it's all really unfortunate."

Almost to the end of the hall, something Gina said finally had enough force to pull Tim away from his mission. He stopped, staring on at the door. He couldn't take his eyes off of it. Something about it made him want to look, made it nearly impossible for him to look away. Gina's words sank in too, though. Something she'd said hanging on a ledge in the corners of his mind. *Her? Her who? Hungry? What does that have to do with anything?*

He shook his head hard. "Wait...what? What were you saying? I'm sorry, I didn't catch what you sai—" A sharp pain radiated into the back of his head and he collapsed onto the floor. His vision blurry, he thought he caught a glimpse of a short, cute girl above him for a brief second, and the only person he could think of in that moment was Gina. "Hold on... whas—" he mumbled, as he saw the young lady raise a foot into the air and bring it down on his face.

§

When Tim woke up, he was lying on a hard surface in a dark room. He could smell the mildew again, stronger than before, and the feeling of something tight against his wrists and ankles registered immediately.

"Wh...what the...hey! Hello? Gina? Somebody? What's going on? What is this?"

A metallic sound rang from his left side, and suddenly, the room was filled with a bright light as a door opened.

"Goddamn," he shouted, the beam of light shining straight into his eyes. "Gina? Is that you? What the fuck is going on? If this is some kind of fucked up prank, you better stop it right now! It's not funny!"

"A prank?" Gina said with a laugh. "Oh, I wish it was a prank. But, unfortunately for you, it's all too real."

He tried to roll over, but the restraints prevented any movement. "What the fuck is going on?" he yelled out as he started to cry. "I didn't do anything to you!"

"I know, Tim. I know you didn't. You see, though, you and your mom are new in town, no relatives that know where you are. You're an only child. It's really easier when they're like you. A lot less to worry about in the long run."

"What are you talking about," he shouted, tears flowing freely now.

"Listen," Gina said. "For what it's worth, I really am sorry about all this. It's not like I have a choice in any of it. I really do like you, or, I *did* like you, I suppose is the best way to phrase it at this point. You really seem like a good guy, and you seriously do have a great sense of humor."

"You don't have to do this, though! Just let me go, please?"

"I *do* have to do it. I'm the only one who can. She won't tolerate anyone else. She's my great-great-grandmother, after all, and she barely tolerates me. I've helped her spill *so much* blood, Tim. Too much. But she has to eat. She *has* to. If we don't feed her...if *I* don't feed her...well, she'll come for us, for everyone. The children first, then the parents. She doesn't care about anyone here. The forests will die, there won't be any more crops. I tried to tell you before, she's very powerful. You found the footprints of the others we brought to her. Those that we fed to her. I thought you were gonna walk on in here without any trouble. But you started thinking, and we couldn't have that. There's just too much to risk for the town. It's the whole, 'sacrifice one for the good of the many' argument. You understand, I'm sure. You're a smart guy."

"No! Let me go!" he screamed, snot flinging from his face as he shook his head like an angry dog. "Please? Just...just let me go now and I won't say a thing to anyone! I swear!"

Gina laughed, then checked her watch. Ten twenty-four. "I'm sorry. I don't mean to laugh. It's just that, I can't let you go, even though I *really* want to."

A dark shadow filled the room, despite the beam of the flashlight shining directly into it. At first, Tim thought that someone else with another light was walking toward him from the other side of the room, but when he turned to look, there wasn't anything there. Instead, against the wall where Gina's light shined, a dark mass began to spread. It looked like a shadow, but it was forming on the wall itself, spreading to places where the light didn't even ouch. It was darker than the night, something that, in spite of everything else that was happening, gave Tim a very unsettling feeling.

He turned back to Gina one last time, begging for her to set him free, but she was gone. In her place sat a chair, the flashlight perched atop it, shining into the room. The figure from the wall was above him now, and it was taking the shape of a woman. There were no features, no eyes or mouth, just a coal black mass, something that looked like the shadow of a shadow, if such a thing ever existed.

There was no sound coming from it, no smell, just an eerily calming movement, graceful almost, as it glided across the surfaces of the room and took its final humanoid shape. Tim was crying uncontrollably now, his words lost in a jumble of strange sounds that no person could decipher. He looked up at the ceiling, watching as an even darker blob took form in what could only be the face of the shadowy thing. He opened his mouth to scream, to cry for his life as loud as he could, but that cry would not come.

As he took in one deep and final breath, the newly formed mouth of the shadowy spirit opened wide and fell from above, consuming Tim in one swift motion.

THE ANNUAL SOIREE

LEO MASSAGED THE BACK OF HIS NECK, THANKFUL THE meeting was finally over. His brow glistened with a light layer of sweat, and he used the cuff of his sleeve to wipe it away. All the worry had been for nothing.

George saw him come out of the conference room, waited for Mr. Jones to get out of sight, and rushed over. "Well?"

Leo looked at him with a puzzled look. "Well, what?"

"Come on, man. Don't do this to me. You know what I'm talking about. How did it go? Did Mr. Jones ream you?" He pulled Leo into the break room next to the water cooler. "Come on, spill!"

"Oh, the meeting?" he said, laughing. "It went...well... actually. Yeah, it went pretty damn good." He smiled, continued to massage his neck. "It was the strangest thing, though. He told me that I'd been doing great work since I've been here, and that he saw a lot of potential in me."

George opened a snack cake from the vending machine and stuffed it into his mouth. "Really? That's good." He swallowed and wiped crumbs from the corners of his lips. "Nothing strange about that, though. You *do* turn out great work. I've seen it. Better than most of what *I've* done, and I've been here for years."

"Yeah, but, there's something else." He chuckled and poured a cup of water from the cooler. "He invited me to this thing on Friday night. I don't know, some kind of private party or something. Just seems weird to me."

George took a deep breath and choked on his snack. "What? He invited *you*? That's great, Leo!"

"Great? How you figure that? It's just a party, man. Honestly, I kinda wish he hadn't invited me. Not like I wanna go or anything...but now I feel like I have to."

"Leo! This is his annual soiree. His *bigshot* party. He throws one every summer. Well, I mean, *I've* never been, but still, it's a good thing! In fact, come to think of it, nobody that's still working here or in this office has been. But that's because those that do go are set for life."

Eyes squinted, Leo's hand found his chin. "Set? What do you mean, set?"

"Look, they say these parties are more like interviews. And not just the ordinary kind. I'm talking interviews where the job at hand is already filled, by the person from this office that gets invited. Catch my drift?"

"Oh, you're crazy. There's gonna be a ton of people there. It's just a party, not an interview."

"That's where you're wrong. It's just him and a handful of his big wig rich buddies. Kinda like a gentleman's club or something. I've been here for five years now, and each year, the guy or gal he invites gets hired on by some well to do firm that pays buckets of money."

"Really? But what would he wanna give me an opportunity like that for? I haven't even been here for a year. He's not had time to develop an opinion of me yet. Not a real one, anyway."

George placed his hand on Leo's shoulder, shook it gently, and grinned. "Look, buddy. It isn't ours to question why. It's only ours to take big opportunities, get big raises, and not bitch and whine when offered free promotions."

"But, it just doesn't make any sense. Are you sure? I mean..."

George pulled out his phone and unlocked the screen. "Like I said, every summer Mr. Jones throws one of these things. And every year, the person he invites jumps ship and joins some big firm up in New York." He fiddled around with his phone, incessantly swiping the screen. "Ah! Here it is. Look at this." He handed the phone to Leo.

"Okay...and?"

"You see that guy? That's Ben Jacobs. He used to work here. Lasted less than a year, kinda like you. I follow his social media. Look at where he works *now*."

Leo pinched the screen and zoomed in. "Lambert and Stevens? Wh-what's that?"

"That's where you're gonna be after Friday night."

Leo looked off into the distance. "I don't know about all that."

"Look, Leo, it's a done deal, I'm telling you. Like I said, Ben was here for less than a year, and I know for a *fact* that the quality of *your* work is better than his ever was. I'm tellin' ya, buddy. You're set."

§

Leo pulled up to Mr. Jones's house fifteen minutes before he was supposed to arrive. He parked on the street, hoping to stay out of sight. His palms were sweaty, so he wiped them against his pants, turned off the headlights, and leaned back in the seat. He watched as the guests arrived, one by one, each driving a fancier car than the last. He shook his head. "George is crazy. I don't belong here. To hell with this." He inserted the key, readying himself to leave, but just as he started to turn it, his phone vibrated.

"Great. It's Mr. Jones." Leo glanced back up at the house, his phone still vibrating, and swiped the screen. "Hello?" A quiet that seemed to last for ages fell over the phone, the raspy drag of heavy breathing the only sound he could hear. "Uh, h-hello?"

A strong and steady voice replied. "Hello, Leo. We're ready now."

"Huh? Ready? Oh, you mean for the—"

"Look up, Leo. Second story, all the way to your right."

His eyes widened, the phone slowly drifted away from his ear. A dark figure, no more than a shadow cast against the light radiating from the room, waved at him from the house.

"Mr. Jones?"

"We're ready now, Leo. This is a grand opportunity for someone like you. Are you ready to embrace it?"

His heart accelerated, his breathing rapid and shallow. It wasn't as if he'd done anything wrong, but the feeling of being *found out*, of being *discovered*, like a thief casing a house before they smashed the windows in and robbed the owners blind, engulfed him.

"Oh, uh, I didn't mean to...I mean, it's not what it looks like."

"Relax, Leo. We knew you were here. Let us help you inside."

"I don't think I need any he—"

The driver's side door opened and Leo jerked up in his seat, his head thumping against the roof of the car. "What the hell?"

Two men dressed in black suits stood in front of him, empty and emotionless expressions on their faces.

"They're here to assist you, Leo. Let them help you. Let them do their job."

"Help me? But I told you, I don't need any—"

"It's a very large house. We wouldn't want you to get lost."

The larger of the two men reached out. "I'll take that now."

Confused, Leo let out a nervous chuckled. "Take what, my phone?" He moved back, away from the men. "I don't think so."

"Let them have it, Leo," Mr. Jones said. "It's for my safety. I'm a very rich man, you know, and my private life is very... personal. I'm not saying that you would, but I don't know you *that* well, now do I?"

"You're afraid I'm gonna steal somethin'? Look man, I'm not some kind of weirdo or thief."

"Give it to them, Leo. Otherwise, they'll have to take it. And they can be very persuasive, if you get my drift."

He looked up at the window again. The dark figure remained, unmoving. He looked to the men outside his car. They stood strong, still, waiting patiently for his compliance.

"The phone, please?"

"Don't worry, Leo. Everyone has to surrender theirs, too. You'll have it back as soon as this is over with. I assure you."

"If you say so. Not like I have a choice, it seems." He hung up with Mr. Jones and handed the phone to the man. As he stepped out of the car, a sudden sense of loneliness came over him. The sensation was strong, causing his stomach to churn like a rolling wave in the ocean during a massive storm. He looked to the window again. The shadowy figure had disappeared.

Something was off. Something didn't *feel* right.

I should have just stayed at the fucking house.

A man on each side of Leo helped to escort him up the long drive and onto the sidewalk. They were quiet, a near deafening silence filling the spaces between them. As they approached the stoop, the man to his right stopped and placed his hand to his ear.

"Yes, sir. I understand. I'll let him know."

Leo turned to him, his left arm restricted by the grip of the other man. "Let me know what? You were talking about me, I assume?"

The man looked at the goon on the other side of Leo and nodded. "It's almost time. Get ready."

"Almost time? For what? Jesus, man. What's going on here?"

Leo felt their grips tighten around his arms, a squeezing pain radiated up into both shoulders. "Hey, get off of me! What the fuck is this?"

"Stay calm," one of them said. "It's easier when you stay calm."

"Stay calm? What's going o—" The front door opened, drawing Leo's attention. "Holy shit!"

In front of him stood a large man, naked from the neck down. His body hairless, the image of a goat tattooed on his chest, the entire outline filled in with coal black ink; a stark contrast against his blindingly white skin. His head replaced by the severed head of a bull, it's eyes removed to form deep, cavernous pits that seemed to be filled with emptiness. Behind the man, a large crowd, all wearing similar masks, roared.

Leo began to shake uncontrollably. He jerked and fought to free himself from the grip of the two henchmen, but it was no use. "What in the hell is this?"

The man at the door stretched his arms out and waved, gesturing for Leo to follow. "Come, Leo. It's time. We've been waiting for you patiently."

"Mr. Jones? I…is that *you*?"

All of a sudden, Leo felt something slip around his neck, tightening around his throat with blinding speed.

"H-Hey!"

The pressure grew stronger.

"L-let m…"

His vision began to fade away, until finally, full on black, and darkness consumed the light.

§

Leo woke to the feeling of icy steel against his groin. His eyes unfocused, he moved to sit up, but something held him back. He jerked his hands, his feet, but he quickly realized that straps had beel placed around his wrists and ankles that prevented his freedom.

"Hey, what's going on?"

"Leo!" Mr. Jones yelled, the bull head muffling his voice. "Thank you for coming. For a moment, I was afraid you wouldn't show."

"Mr. Jones? What are you—"

"I'm sorry to be the bearer of bad news, Leo. But you've been chosen for this year's annual ritual. You're the only one left who doesn't have a family; the only one who won't be *missed*." He walked around Leo's body, from his feet to his head, and stared down into his eyes. "Years ago, our ancestors entered into a sacred pact with one known simply as, The Bargainer."

His head moving erratically, tears formed in the corners of his eyes. "This has got to be some kind of sick joke! You...you're hazing me...i-is that it?"

"In exchange for eternal wealth and power, The Bargainer asks for one thing, and one thing only." He raised the knife over Leo's face, allowing full view of the shiny blade. "It's simple, and it's easy. He requires a sacrifice."

"No," Leo said, shaking his head in protest. "This is a joke. Tell me now, this is all just a sick, fucking joke, isn't it? George told me...Ben's social media page, i-it says he works for—"

"Tonight, you will provide us with this service." He lowered the blade onto Leo's cheek and carved a long, deep incision.

"Jesus fucking Christ!"

"I'm afraid not, Leo. You're in the wrong place for him."

Laughter roared from the crowd as they formed a circle around the table.

Mr. Jones took a cup and placed it against Leo's face. "We take thy blood to cleanse our bodies." Blood began to collect in the cup as a dark, crimson stain spread across the glass. "In the beginning, thou shall drink!"

The crowd cheered.

"No! Please?"

The two men from the car came to his side, each wielding a large meat clever.

"We take thy flesh, to feed our hunger, and before our reward, we feast!"

§

George watched anxiously for Mr. Jones to arrive on Monday morning. He saw his car pull into the parking lot and ran to him as he walked through the front door.

"Mr. Jones, sir?"

"Well hello there, George. Is there something I can help you with?"

"No, sir. Well, I mean, I was just curious...I heard your annual soiree was this past weekend. How did it go? I heard, I mean...Leo told me he was invited. Not trying to pry or anything, I was just curious."

Mr. Jones smiled, his eyes filled with contentment. "It's okay, George. No worries. As for the party, we had a great time." He licked his lips, a groan of pleasure fled from deep within his stomach. "Leo had a great time, as well."

The Donkey Tree

JACOB FANNED SMOKE FROM HIS FACE AS HE TRIED TO concentrate on the menu laying on the table in front of him. He fought it as best he could, but with noxious fumes creeping up his nostrils like a centipede crawling into a dark hole, he had no choice.

"I...I can't," he said, eyes narrowing to tiny, thin slits. "I can't t...take it any-m-m...more." He inhaled, paused briefly, and with a loud grunt, sneezed into the crook of his elbow.

"Ha!" Ron yelled, arching backward in his chair as laughter exploded from his lungs. "Now that's what I call a sneeze. You shook the whole damn table!"

"Yeah, that was a rough one."

Ron coughed and waved his hand, fanning the smoke away from his own face. "What is this anyway? The fifties?" He looked around the mostly empty diner. One couple sat in the far corner, and on their left, two tables over, an older man sat alone. They were all puffing away on cigarettes. "It's fucking 2018 for Christ's sake! We know that smoking causes cancer! It's proven! And here, in small town Kentucky, here in *Hicksville*, every fucking hillbilly has a goddamn cigarette."

"Be quiet, Ron. You want to get us thrown out?"

"I don't give a—"

The old man to their left stood from his table and cleared his throat. In a deep, raspy voice, he asked, "you boys got some kinda problem?" He wore bibbed overalls with no shirt underneath and an old, worn baseball cap covered his balding head. The skin on his face sagged heavily, suggesting his age to be upwards of seventy.

His face flushed, Jacob hung his head and stared at the menu. "Uh, no sir. We're, uh...we're sorry."

"I'd appreciate if you'd try to keep it down," the man said. "I'm tryin' to enjoy my lunch."

"Happy now?" Jacob whispered to Ron. "I told you to be quiet."

"I don't give a fuck," Ron said in a hushed voice. "How long did that mechanic say it would take again? I wanna get outta this godforsaken place and back on the fucking road."

"He said it shouldn't take more than a few hours," Jacob answered, raising his hand to flag down the waitress. "I'm not too sure I believe him, though. Didn't really seem like he was all there if you know what I mean."

"Look around, man." Ron peered to his right, then to his left, looking from the corners of his eyes to be as inconspicuous as possible. He saw the old man in overalls, who had taken his seat again after scolding them, and snorted. "Does anybody in this place look like they're all there?"

"Yeah, tell me about it. This place is *definitely* not like Chicago."

"Y'all decide what you'd like?" the server asked as she approached the table.

"Yes ma'am," Jacob replied. "At least I have. I can't speak for him," he said, pointing to Ron.

"I'll figure it out," Ron grumbled. "Just order so we can go."

§

"Well, that killed an entire thirty minutes," Ron said, checking his phone for the time. "Three hours, huh? Jesus, what are we supposed to do in this place for two and a half more hours?"

Jacob took the last bite of his meatloaf and scooted his plate away as their server brought them the bill.

"Here y'all go. Was everything good?"

"Absolutely," Jacob replied, laying the money for the check down in front of her. "Best meatloaf I've ever eaten." He arched back and patted his stomach to show his contentment with the food. "Say, you from around this area?"

"Easy now, Jacob," Ron said, looking the young girl up and down. "We're not gonna be here *that* long."

The young lady's brow furrowed, but she forced a smile. Dealing with comments like this was, unfortunately, part of the job, but that didn't mean she liked them. She looked back at Jacob. "Yeah. Grew up here. Somethin' I can help y'all find?"

"Well," he said chuckling. "I'm not real sure. You see, we're from Chicago and we're on our way to Panama City for spring break. Our car broke down a few miles from here and this was the closest town that had a garage."

"Ha, if you can call that place a garage," Ron interjected.

Jacob cast a disapproving look his way before continuing. "According to the mechanic, it's gonna be awhile. We were sort of looking for something to do to pass the time. You wouldn't have any suggestions, would you? Is there anything to do around here for fun?"

"You mean like the movies or somethin'?"

"Jesus Christ," Ron said. "He means *anything*. Movies, bowling, a damn bar. Literally anything at all to kill a few hours."

"Ron, be nice."

He shook his head and leaned back in his chair.

Jacob looked back to the server with sympathy in his eyes. "I'm sorry, ma'am. We're just tired. He didn't mean anything."

Ron snorted and raised his eyebrow as he mumbled under breath.

The young lady cocked her head and smiled politely. "I'm sorry, fellas. Ain't nothin' like that 'round here. Why, this ain't the *big city*, after all. I guess we're just a little hick town." She grabbed the cash, stuffed it in her pocket, and walked back toward the kitchen.

"How do you like that? She didn't even give us the change," Ron said.

"Don't worry about it. It's her tip."

"Yeah, sure. She probably can't even count."

"You're an asshole, you know that, Ron?"

The old man in overalls next to them stood again. His knees popped and cracked as he made his way to their table. He stood in front of the boys, thumbs resting on his bibs, his lips moved back and forth as if they were in a constant state of puckering and unpuckering.

"Great," Ron mumbled. "Father Time's back greet us once more."

The old man looked down at them as if he were about to scold them for stealing the last of the cookies from the jar at their grandparent's house. "You boys is awful loud. Sounded like you's lookin' for somethin' to do for a bit. That about right?"

Jacob laughed nervously. "Uh, I mean, sure. We're gonna

be here for a bit. Might as well make the best of it, right?"

"I'll be honest with you. I don't much like the way y'all treated Mary. She's a good girl, and the way y'all talked to her," the man shifted his feet, nodded his head toward Ron, "especially you, it was just plain disrespectful."

"Uhm...I'm *sorry*?" Ron said, one eyebrow raised.

"Mhm, I know you are. Sorry as fuck." He focused his attention back on Jacob. "Down here, parents try to teach their kids how to be nice. Respectful. That's somethin' y'all could use some work on."

"Look, sir, we didn't mean anything by it. My friend, he's just tired. I'll go apologize to her for the both of us," Jacob said, trying to avoid any further conflict.

"Damage's already done. I'd say it'd be best for you boys to just go somewhere else before somebody says or does somethin' they might regret. You get my drift?"

Jacob looked to Ron, then back to the old man, his eyes squinted. "I'm not sure, but let me see if I do. Are you *threatening* us?"

The old man stood firm; eyes locked with Jacob's. "I'm just sayin' that when boys like you come into places like this lookin' for somethin' to do, sometimes they get a little more than they bargained for."

Having heard enough of what he was sure was just crazy old man talk from some Kentucky fried redneck, Ron's short temper got the best of him. "Look old timer," he said, standing to his feet and placing his hand on the old man's shoulder. "Believe it or not, I've been nice up until now. I've been *really* nice. Now, it's been a rough day. I'm tired, my friend's tired, so don't push it, okay?"

"Manners, boy. I wasn't finished talkin' just yet." The old man reached his hand up and smacked Ron's arm in an attempt to move it from his shoulder, but it didn't budge; the pressure was too much.

"Now, since you want us out of your way so bad, and trust me, I'd love nothing more than to leave this place, too, surely you know a somewhere we could go until our car is fixed, right?"

"Ron, leave him alone. He looks serious."

"Oh, I'm serious, too." Ron squeezed the man's arm, his grip tightening until his fist quivered. "What do you say, old-timer? Like you said, wouldn't wanna do anything or say anything that might end up getting someone hurt, now would we?"

"Ron, seriously. You're gonna get us—"

The server came back out of the kitchen with a baseball bat in hand. "It's time for you boys to get on outta here before I call the law." She made her way toward them as she raised the bat overhead, ready to swing it down at an instant.

The old man raised his free hand and waved her away. "They was doin' just that, Mary. I was just about to tell 'em 'bout the donkey tree."

"O...oh," she replied, freezing mid-step. "The donkey tree?" Her face turned pale, her voice dropped both in tone and volume, like all the wind had been knocked out of her.

"Yeah. I figure that'll keep 'em busy for long enough." He shrugged his arm, fighting the painful squeeze.

Like a snake releasing its prey, Ron let go of the man's arm causing him to stumble backward into a table. "Ha! The donkey tree, huh?" He turned toward Jacob and laughed. "You hear that? These people have a tree named after a donkey!"

Jacob, face red with embarrassment, tossed another twenty dollars on the table. "I'm sorry, really. I hope this helps...for your troubles, you know?"

Ron looked at the old man and laughed. "Well, what the fuck is a donkey tree?"

§

A light drizzle forced the fugitive dust particles into submission as Ron and Jacob made their way up the old dirt road. The air held a light chill, and their rain-soaked clothes weren't helping.

"That old bastard's a fucking idiot," Ron said, stuffing his hands into his pockets. "I'll bet he made that whole thing up just to get rid of us. Did you see how scared he was?"

Jacob walked next to him; his arms crossed tightly against his body to conserve warmth. "Would you blame him? You were being a pretty big asshole back there."

"Me? Why, I was just joking around with him. It's not my fault these southern fuck heads can't take a goddamn joke. Though, if that tree isn't out here and he caused me to get wet for nothing, I *will* go back and kick his old ass just to teach him a lesson."

"It's out here. I'd almost bet on it. Just a matter of finding it."

"Really? You think there's actually something called a donkey tree out here? A *magic* donkey tree to be exact?"

"I don't know, but it's one hell of a story to just make up on the spot. Don't you think? I mean, a magic tree in the shape of a donkey with the power to curse or bring good fortune? That's pretty intense."

"Yeah, I guess so. But then again, you gotta remember who told it in the first place."

"That's true. There was something about the way that server looked when he mentioned it, though. It was almost like she was afraid of it. Nah, I'd say it's out here. Probably some kind of story they use to scare little kids on Halloween. Like you said, they gotta do something for fun."

Ron stopped in the middle of the road, checked his watch, and sighed. "Jesus. We've been walking for nearly half an hour. I'm wet, cold, and about ready to just say fuck it. This old man's a damn—"

"Ron, look!" Jacob said, grabbing his friend's arm. "There it is. That has to be it, right?" He twisted Ron to the right and pointed out into the middle of a large hay field. "It looks just like he said."

"Well, I'll be. It's a *goddamn* donkey tree." Ron jogged to the edge of the field and hopped over a small ditch into the grass. "We've come this far in the rain. Might as well go see it, huh?"

Jacob glanced down at his dirty shoes. They were covered in mud from a combination of rain and road grit. He shrugged his shoulders. "Let's do it."

A normal sized tree compared to others in the bordering woods, the donkey tree stood at least twenty feet in height. The trunk was split into two branches. The first was straight, but the second bared a large knot about five feet from the ground that pushed down and outward, giving it the crude shape of a donkey's face. Atop the knot, the trunk split again into two smaller limbs that resembled ears. On top of each section, bright green foliage burst from bud tips, adding the look of hair to the beast.

"Wow," Jacob gasped. "It really does look like a donkey. That's amazing."

"It's something, alright," Ron mocked. "And this thing is supposed to bring us good luck?"

Jacob leaned in and touched the nose of the wooden animal, feeling inside a small hole at its tip. "This is supposed to be the mouth, I think. That's going off what the old man said, anyway. Something about putting an apple in there. You know, donkeys like to eat apples...don't they?"

"How am I supposed to know? Do I look like a fucking donkeyologist to you? Besides, I don't have any apples. I have something else I can give it, though." Ron stepped up against the tree and unzipped his pants.

"Come on, man. Don't you think you've caused enough trouble around here? What if somebody passing by sees you?"

Ron's head twisted to one side, then to the other. "Yeah. This place is packed to the gills with people," he said, sarcasm filling his voice. "Besides, I'll bet this poor guy hasn't had anything other than rainwater to drink for God knows how long. He could use a little lemonade. If it'll make you feel better though, you can keep watch for me. Be a lookout or some shit."

A hot stream of piss splatted against the tree's trunk and soaked into the ground at its base. Jacob stood behind, looking up and down the road in hopes that one of the locals didn't see what was happening and decide to come out with a twelve-gauge shotgun to blow them to bits.

"Hurry, man. Drain that thing and let's get out of here."

Ron moaned and placed one hand on the donkey tree for support. "What's the hurry, huh? You see somebody or something?"

"No, but I don't wanna take any—"

"Wait," Ron interrupted. "What was that?" He leaned into the tree harder to catch his balance and zipped up. "Did you hear it?"

Jacob stood with his arms stretched out to his sides. "I didn't hear anything, but I sure as hell felt something. It was like some kind of weird shake or tremor."

Beneath their feet, the ground began to vibrate. It wasn't much at first, definitely not enough to cause immediate alarm, but it *was* enough that they both felt it; enough to leave no room for doubt.

"Is it an earthquake? Do they have those here?" Ron asked.

"I don't think so."

The vibrations intensified and a small crack began to open in the ground between them. Above, a light wind rose up as if they were being fanned from the heavens. As they fought to stay upright, they each looked toward the sky and saw the young branches of the donkey tree swaying back and forth. Jacob turned, followed by Ron, and what they saw sent a shock deep into their very core; a shock that was ten times what that of any earthquake would have been capable of.

"Holy fuck!" Ron yelled. "I...it's—"

Knees buckling, Jacob fell backward on his ass in awe. "It's the donkey tree! I-i-it's moving!"

Like something straight out of a nightmare, the donkey tree ripped from the earth, massive bundles of roots twirling together to form thick, gargantuan, elephant-like legs. The straightest branch of the tree curled downward to form the back half of its body and tail while the deformed branch elongated to form the rest of the body and face.

"This can't be happening!" Ron screamed. "Ww...we gotta go, Jacob. We gotta go, now!"

He reached for his friend to help him up, and they bolted in a dead sprint toward the road. Behind them, they heard the donkey tree running, galloping after them. Each strike of its deformed root wad hooves made a loud, thunderous clop, sinking into the ground and sending tiny bits of earth into the air.

"What the hell is that thing!" Jacob called out as he gasped for breath.

"Don't stop running!" Ron replied in long, painful heaves.

As they neared the road, the donkey tree bellowed, releasing a piercing scream, its force powerful enough to send Jacob and Ron face first into the mud.

"No, we've gotta get up, man. We've gotta go!" Ron said, his feeble attempts at getting a hold in the slippery conditions failing.

Jacob rolled onto his back, his chest now covered in thick, slimy brown sludge. "This can't be real!"

They kicked and clawed at the soil; their limbs unable to gain purchase as the donkey tree gained ground on them. Rain continued to fall and their cries for help went unheard as they begged for someone, *anyone*, to save them from this horrible nightmare. They pushed and squirmed at the soft mud, legs and arms burning in pain as their spent muscles screamed for more oxygen.

Jacob's fingers hurt, the cold seared into his joints like ice, and just when he thought it was no use, Jacob's nails dug into something solid. He flung his face up and saw that he'd finally reached the edge of the road. "Ron, grab my leg," he yelled, gripping the solid ground as best he could. "I'll pull us out!" Just as he felt his friend's hands wrap around his leg, the ground erupted in a vicious quake as the donkey tree leapt into the air and landed above them, its legs straddling their tired bodies.

With a deep, painful moan, the donkey tree let out a vicious, unworldly cry. It was a sound so full of grief and terror that even the surrounding vegetation seemed to shudder in fear.

Jacob turned his head to see the donkey tree's face above his friend, its leafy ears swaying above its large wooden head.

"Heeee Haaaawww," it bellowed, a wind exiting its mouth with a force so strong that it blew chunks of mud from each of their bodies.

"Cars," Ron said, pointing toward the road. "Look, Jacob! We're saved! It's our car!"

Jacob shot a look toward the road, and sure enough, there was their car. Next to it sat an old, worn down pickup truck.

"Easy now," a voice called from the truck as the door flung open. Inside sat the old man from the diner. He slowly got out of the vehicle, laughing with every crooked step. "I reckon they've had about enough."

Like a well-trained dog, the donkey tree reared back on its hind legs and sat still.

Jacob and Ron clambered out of the muddy field and onto the road with a speed that could match that of an Olympic level runner.

"Car!" Ron yelled. "Let us in the car!"

"Not so fast," the old man said, still laughing. "Billy, you can get out, but wait before you give 'em the keys."

A small boy, no more than twelve or fourteen years in age, exited the driver's side of their vehicle.

"You bring 'em?" the old man asked.

Billy nodded and handed a bag of apples to the old man.

"I'd say it's y'alls lucky day," the old man said. "Car's done early. Now you boys remember this, you hear me? Next time you find yourself in a small town like this one, maybe you won't go around hatin' and threatenin' people. You understand?"

Jacob and Ron stood between the vehicles, speechless, and nodded furiously.

"Good. Go ahead and give 'em their keys back, Billy."

The boy tossed Jacob the keys and hopped into the old man's truck.

"B...but, that *thing*, that donkey tree," Ron said.

"What about it?" the old man replied.

"Won't it kill you? Won't it kill everyone?"

"Nah," he replied. "I killed it and buried it right there where it came from 'round about, oh...must've been twenty-five or thirty years back. Goddamn thing just won't stay dead." The old man tossed the bag of apples into the mud and the donkey tree gulped them down immediately. As if commanded by its master, the donkey tree turned and galloped back to the middle of the field. Its roots started burying back into the earth and the trunk contorted back into nothing more than a tree resembling a donkey.

Jacob and Ron stared, eyes wide and mouths hanging open, unable to believe what they had just witnessed.

"He's usually pretty good, as long as you treat him right," the old man said with a smile.

"I don't understand," Jacob said.

"I'd forget about it if I was you and just git on outta here."

The boys looked at each other, unsure of what to do, frozen in a place between what they could only guess to be reality and fantasy.

"Well," the old man yelled. "Go on! Git!"

Not wasting another second, the boys jumped into their car. Jacob slammed it into drive and floored it, skidding on the wet road as they left the town and its donkey tree behind them forever.

BIG DADDY

"WHA' Y'ALL-A-DOIN' DOWN IN 'ERE?"

James was silent for a moment as he stared back at the man. It wasn't that he didn't know how to answer or what to say. He'd been doing this kind of work for a long time, and he'd dealt with all different types of people. Even though his job was a bit unique...or, at least it wasn't a job that you hear about often, making it kind of hard to explain...he'd learned how to explain it well. So that wasn't the problem at all. This, rather, was a case of not wanting to say the wrong thing and potentially get both him and his assistant, Melissa, shot on site. That, he'd reasoned many times in his life, is never an accepted or desired outcome.

"Well," the man said, mouth hanging open as if he were utterly confused. "Y'all gonna fuckin' answer me or what?"

James thought about it for a second, considering how he could carefully word his answer the man's potential intentions. He had pulled sideways in the middle of the road in front of them to block it, and that usually wasn't a great sign. James looked at the man and the first thing he noticed wasn't the stereotypical bibbed denim overalls with more holes in them than actual material, and it wasn't the old and faded blue baseball cap that looked and smelled like it'd been rolled in a steaming pile of dog shit that sat perched halfway atop his rather bulbous and bald head. Hell, it wasn't even his poorly groomed facial hair, a style that, sadly, reminded James more of the once hairy ass of a mangey animal that someone had taken a pair of dull clippers to while it had diarrhea, all in a drastically failed attempt to make it look better. And, while the look on the man's face was one of shear idiocy, a look that James had honestly expected to see in this area, that wasn't what caught his attention, either.

No, it wasn't any of that...though each and every one of those things easily invited first dibs in any normal, non-West Virginian area.

It was his voice.

There was something off about it, especially when compared to his appearance. A man of this individual's stature, of his rather...*interesting* appearance...should have a voice that's deep and rough, rugged and masculine. Instead, his voice seemed to be stuck several registers higher than what James had imagined it, or any man's, should be. It was nowhere near what any normal individual would consider either rugged or masculine. In fact, it sounded like his balls had started to drop when he was twelve, but instead of finishing like a normal man's would, his had somehow lodged mid-pelvis, leaving him with the ability to compete with professional opera singers as they struggled to hit the highest notes humans could possibly belt out.

And perhaps the most off-putting thing about it, not that all of this wasn't worthy of classifying as off-putting to begin with, was the speed at which he spoke. James could deal with the sound, but the speed was as near to being *too unbearable* as you could get, but still be bearable. He pictured the man starting a sentence, one of less than ten words even, and watching a slug sprint the one-hundred-meter dash before he was even able to get the last word out.

"Goddamnit! I asked y'all a goddamn question ya goddamn sonsofabitches!"

"James," Melissa whispered from the passenger's seat as she slapped his arm. "Answer him, please! He's getting angry!"

James shook his head, his assistant's jolt bringing him out of his own daydream. "Oh, uhm, ye-yeah. I'm sorry." He looked up at the man and stuck his hand out the window. "My name is James Blevins. Didn't mean to catch you off guard. I work for a private consulting firm and we're out here doing some work for the Department of Transportation."

The man looked at him, eyes squinted, deep and raspy breaths in and out that seemed to grow louder with each passing second. "Transportation? Ain't no *goddamn* transportation out in here, goddamnit! What'na hell y'all talkin' 'bout? It look like 'ey's any goddamn blacktop roads out in the middle of 'ese goddamn hills to you? Y'all's a bunch of goddamn morons!"

James chuckled, doing everything he could not to explode in an all-out full-blown laugh. Respect went a long way with people in places like this...places that both time and literacy seemed to have forgotten...and laughing at the man, warranted or not, would most definitely cross that line. "Well, sir, I guess you've got a point on that one. No, there aren't any major roads out here. But..." He turned to Melissa, her young nearly stark white from nerves, and smiled at her. "Reach me the maps."

She handed him a folded sheet of paper and glanced up at the man, the first time she'd made direct eye contact with him.

James unfolded the map and pointed to a highway lined in various colors marking limits of disturbance, new build areas, and all the other engineering bullshit he really had no idea about. "I'm sure you've heard about the proposed work out here on Highway 929, yeah?"

The man leaned in and looked at the map. "'Elp, I reckon I've heard 'bout it." His eyes shifted to James again, a look of skepticism radiating from his eyes. "What's 'at got to do with y'all bein' out here, 'ough? Goddamn highway's half a mile or more from here, goddamnit. Surely to God 'ey ain't gonna try and bring it through *my* woods, are they?"

"No, no. Not at all. That's not why we're here."

"Goddamnit, boy, you just like bein' in the middle of a big ol' goddamn circle jerk or somethin'?" He leaned in, his eyes locking on Melissa. "But 'en, I reckon with 'at perty little thing sittin' over 'ere next to ya, a goddamn circle jerk might be a little bit of fun, ain't it?" He licked his lips, then shifted his attention back to James without missing a beat. "Cause 'at's what y'all's a doin'...jerkin me off and wastin' my goddamn time. *She* might be fun, but I goddamn sure don't wanna be part of no goddamn jerkin' off of *any* kind with you...no offense."

James looked over at Melissa, her brow furrowed, lips quivering. It was obvious she was scared. But who wouldn't be after those kinds of direct and abrasive remarks?

"Uhm...wha—" James started, turning back to the man. But before he could even get a sentence out, he was interrupted.

"Goddamnit, boy. You gonna tell me why y'all's out here fuckin' around in my woods or not?"

James shook his head, more confused now that he could

ever remember being in his life. "Oh...we-well, I mean...what we do is survey for threatened and endangered species. You see, when any kind of federal money is put into play and potential habitat is disturbed, one of the requirements is to conduct surveys for federally listed species in and around the area to be impacted to see if they occur within or adjacent to the proposed project limits."

The man's eyes widened significantly as he inhaled, holding the breath in.

"And around here, that pretty much always means bats."

The man nodded, his posture relaxing a bit. "Bats, huh? Well, you see any fuckin' caves out here?"

"No, but bats don't always live in caves. In fact, most of the bats around here use trees during the summer. And, to get to your original question, *that's* what brings us out here. While the actual road is a half mile or so away, the best habitat to survey for that project is, well...here." He waved his arm, gesturing to the forest in front of them.

"Well goddamn. I don't reckon I've ever heard of nothin' like 'at 'fore, and I still ain't sure 'at's what y'all's a doin' out here...but..." The man stuck his hand out, finally offering a handshake of his own. "Name's RJ. Folks 'round 'ese parts call me Bid Daddy, but you don't know me like 'at, not yet anyways, so y'all can just call me by my God given name. RJ."

James paused, unsure how to respond. "Oh, well, uhm... okay," he said, haking RJ's hand. "Nice to meet you, RJ." He turned to Melissa. "This is Melissa. She helps me conduct the surveys."

RJ leaned over again, getting a better view of Melissa. "Mhm. I seen here earlier, 'member? Said she'd be fun to have as part of a goddamn circle—"

"Hello," she said, cutting RJ off before he could finish. She knew where it was going, and she wanted no part of any other conversations with such content, *especially* from RJ. "It's nice to meet you," she continued, trying to brush off everything that had happened before.

RJ continued to stare. His eyes seemed to narrow slightly and, though it was hard to tell due to the horribly uneven, yet strikingly fitting, patches of course, pubic-like hair that probably passed as both an immaculate mustache and beard in this part of the world, she could see the edges of his lips curl upward to form a sort of perverted smirk. For a moment, she couldn't tell if he was angry or just a creep. She was used to men acting like complete and total jackasses around her, and usually she didn't think much of it. She *was* pretty cute, after all, and she knew that almost all guys were morons. She also knew that most of them are harmless, even if they *are* perverted children a majority of the time. But RJ seemed different. The way he stared, giving off a very primitive and almost aggressive vibe, made her very uncomfortable. She looked away, hoping RJ would get the hint.

He grunted, then chuckled, arching his eyebrows at the same time.

"Anyway," James said, leaning forward to place himself directly in RJ's line of sight and block his view of Melissa. "We just saw this road on a map and thought it may be a decent place to net. We didn't mean to bother you. We'll just be on our way now."

"Mhm," RJ replied. "If you didn't mean to bother me you wouldn't be out here right now fuckin' botherin' me, would ya?" He stood up straight, arching his back to appear as large as possible. He was a rather tall and somewhat portly man, something that became apparent as he hooked his thumbs over the bibs of his overalls and jutted his belly out. "'Is *is* my property, ya know?"

James knew better. This was clearly a public road, after all. An unpaved dirt one, but still public. Though, that wasn't so uncommon deep in Appalachia. But, truth aside, he also knew, based on past experiences working in such areas, that in this sort of place, everything, public or not, was owned by one of two people. The person you were talking to, or their grandpa. In this case, and unfortunately for James and Melissa, this obviously public county road belonged to RJ. And, as luck would have it, his truck just so happened to be blocking the path forward.

"Well," James said, glancing in the rearview mirror to judge whether or not he'd be able to back up to a spot wide enough so that he could turn around. "I mean, we thought this was a public road. It's named on the map. County Road 25, in fact." He turned away from the mirror and rested his elbow in the open window, leaning forward as he looked at RJ.

"Is 'at right?" His head cocked to the side slightly, tongue slipping between chapped lips wetting them just enough that they glistened in the mid-afternoon sunshine. "I bet you don't talk to your mamma with a smartass mouth like 'at, do you?"

James felt a surge of adrenaline course through his veins. Somehow the conversation had went from civil and normal, to completely inappropriate, to something that he felt, and he knew Melissa was feeling too based on her demeanor, dangerous in a matter of seconds.

He forced a nervous smile, hoping it would help deescalate whatever was happening here. "Listen...we didn't mean to bother you or..." he cleared his throat, unable to avoid the opportunity to be passive-aggressive, even under potentially dangerous circumstances. "Well...trespass...so if it's all the same to you, we'll just be on our way and you won't ever have to worry about seeing us again. How's that sound?" He put one hand on the steering wheel, the other on the gear shift, and pressed the brake down as he readied to put the truck in gear.

RJ took a step toward the truck and laid his hand on the door in the still open window. "You wait just a minute, boy."

James watched as RJ's other hand fumbled around in his fanny pack. He knew something was about to happen, he just wasn't sure what.

"J-James," Melissa said in low voice.

He heard her words, but his focus was on RJ's other hand.

"James," she repeated, louder. "They're coming..."

RJ's hand was emerging from the fanny pack, albeit at an abysmally slow pace, a pace that came close to rivaling that of his speech. James could tell he was holding something now, and as it came into view, a glint of sunlight reflecting off a piece of black and shiny steel gave its identity away.

"James!" Melissa cried from the passenger seat. "They're behind us! We have to go *now*!"

James suddenly felt her grab his shoulder and shake him, commanding his attention, which was now on the handgun RJ was slowly bringing up in his face. In any normal situation, James would've thought that the adrenaline was causing RJ's actions to *seem* like they were happening in slow motion, but he knew that wasn't the case here. RJ was just slow as absolute fuck. Quickly, he glanced in the review mirror and saw another truck parked behind them, about one hundred feet back, and two wild and wooly characters were coming up on them at a more normal speed.

He looked back to RJ, the gun finally out of the fanny pack but still far from being pointed in any direction that would cause them harm. He turned to Melissa and shouted, "hold on!", as he threw the truck into reverse and floored the gas.

The two men jumped to either side of the narrow dirt road, one of them falling over the steep slope to the left, the other jumping up onto the steep slope to the right. He took one final look toward RJ and saw that he was *finally* getting the gun held in front of him enough that any bullets shot would at least have a chance at finding their intended target. As James neared the other truck, he glanced to Melissa. "Brace yourself, we have to hit it and hope it pushes out of the way enough that we can get through!" He knew this was the only way. The slope on either side of the road was too steep to navigate, and the drop to the left was a dangerous one. "Hold o—"

Before he could finish, the sound of metal crunching against metal echoed throughout the forest as the ass end of James's truck crashed into the front side of the one blocking the road. He saw Melissa's head slam into the back of her seat and then fling forward into the airbag, finally smacking into the passenger door window with a hard thud. The back window shattered, and as glass flew from behind them, a sudden explosion of pain radiated through James's head. He'd felt it hit something, presumably his own seat, and less than a split second later, his vision went black.

§

James woke to a sudden splash of iciness across his face. He screamed, his eyes springing open as he reflexively gasped for air. "Wha-what the fuck?" He was laying on his face in a puddle of water, but he could feel his feet planted firmly on the ground. He shifted slightly, trying to turn so that he could push himself up to a standing position, but his arms wouldn't move. Instead, he felt something scratchy rubbing against each wrist.

"What the...help! Someone, help me!" James tried to raise up, but just as his wrists had been restrained, he felt a similar sensation across his shoulder blades that kept him from standing. "Hello? What's going..."

He paused for a moment, a sound echoing somewhere in the distance. Somewhere behind a closed door, maybe? High pitched whines? Whimpers? His eyes widened as he took in a deep breath, the realization coming at him with full force.

Melissa?

He raised his head and looked to either side. There was nothing, no one. The only thing he could tell at this point was that it seemed as though someone had tied him down to a wooden table and apparently poured a bucket of water on his head to wake him. In front of the table, directly in front of James's head, sat a chair. It was nothing fancy, just an old and worn folding chair.

The sound came again, only sharper this time, and he could tell without a doubt that it was a woman screaming. "Melissa?" he yelled out. "Are you okay? What are they do—" Another splash of cold water poured over his head catching him off guard. "Goddamn! What the...who the fuck is doing that?" he screamed, shaking his head like a wet dog shakes it's body in the rain. "Melissa!"

"Ain't no sense in you hollerin' like at, boy. Why, she can't hear ya no ways."

James froze. Up until now he'd thought himself alone, but he couldn't see behind him. He couldn't see any farther that what was immediately beside him. He didn't have to see, though, in order to know who it was. There wasn't anyone else on the face of this earth that he was aware of that spoke with such sluggish intent. "RJ? Is that you?"

"How'd ya ever guess? Goddamn, you's smarter 'an I goddamn thought, goddamnit."

James thought about telling him exactly how he knew it was him, but he figured that any sort of smartass crack at this point *definitely* wouldn't help him get out of whatever fucked up situation he'd gotten himself into. "What are you doing? What do you want?"

RJ began to laugh. "What was it you said y'all was up here doin' again? Chasin'...*bats*...was it?"

"Yes," James said. "We didn't mean to trespass! That's all we were doing. I swear!"

"Is 'at right? Well, I don't believe 'at for a second. In fact, I believe 'at y'all's a workin' for the goddamn state DNR. 'At stands for the Division of Natural Resources."

"The DN...I fucking know what it stands for you moron! Why would you even say that to someone you're accusing of working for them? Wouldn't you expect them to...you know what? Never mind. It doesn't matter. I told you; we work for a private consulting firm you fucking halfwit! Jesus fucking Christ, you stupid goddamn hillbilly!"

The room fell silent, the only sounds heard were the distant screams of his assistant in a room somewhere else. Then, he heard the slow creaking of floorboards coming around the sides of the table. Out of his periphery, he caught a glimpse of a thick but firm flesh colored appendage, slowly coming into his field of vision. At a speed not dissimilar to that of his speech, he watched as RJ gradually came into view. He was fully naked now, one hand held over his crotch to block his penis, the other over his chest to block his sagging man titties from view like a shy and timid school girl in a cheap porn.

James gasped, turned his face in the other direction. Goddamnit, man! What the actual *fuck*?"

"Don't you worry 'bout me, boy. 'Is ain't for you noways. I told you back when you was in 'at truck 'at I ain't interested in no circle jerk unless 'at perty little thing you had with you was in it."

"Melissa? What have you done with her?" James yelled, struggling to free himself from his restraints. "I swear to god if you—"

Mid-sentence, James froze as the sound of a door flinging open and slamming against the wall rang out. He twisted his head in the direction of the noise, but he couldn't turn far enough. A series of loud, animal like grunts filled the air, accompanied by the faint whimpers and moans of a woman. James began to panic. They'd killed Melissa, or even worse. Based on the screams and the fact that RJ was standing before him, naked, they'd likely raped her first. He had to do something, had to get out of there, get help.

"No, goddamnit," RJ shouted.

James faced him and turned to see that he was pointing

somewhere behind him, a spot James himself couldn't see.

"Not right 'ere you goddamn dumbasses. Drag her over here. I want 'is un to see her while y'all do the dirty."

"What the fuck?" James said, nervous, confused, fucking scared shitless.

RJ laughed. "'At's right. You see, I know y'all workin' for the DNR. Y'all heard somebody talk 'bout my bigfoots, didn't ya?"

"Bigfo...what?"

"Mhm. 'Em sonsofabitches've been tryin' to find him in 'ese woods for years. They even put a bounty on him. Ten million dollars if you can catch him alive." He smirked. "Bats. Ha! You stupid government bastards gotta goddamn come up with somethin' better'n'at to fool ol' RJ. I've been around, goddamnit. I know things."

James saw RJ point to the floor in front of him, and as he did, a massive, muscular, ape-like creature appeared. It stood on two legs and was at least eight feet high. It was covered in long hair from head to toe, and it's face seemed to have a constant scowl.

"Well, all I can say is, y'all gonna have to do a lot better'n'at to get my bigfoots."

"Th...this is fucking crazy! Absolutely fucking insane!" James cried. "What is happening to me?"

The creature walked over to RJ, who had taken a step back and sat in the chair, leaned over, and gave him one of the longest, nastiest, sloppiest tongue kisses he'd ever seen anyone give. It reached its hand down and fondled RJ's cock, gently caressing his miniscule balls before pulling away from him.

"This isn't real," James said out loud. "This isn't fucking *real!*"

"Oh, it's real all right. And you're about to experience it all for yourself. Ya see...I ain't gonna stand by and let the government fuck ol' RJ. No sir. RJ's the one who does the fuckin' 'round 'ese woods, goddamnit. Or, in 'is case, they do the fuckin'."

"Th...oh no..."

Just then, another of the creatures walked into view, dragging Melissa by the hair. It stood in front of him for a moment, then dropped Melissa on the ground. She wasn't dead, that much he could tell by her twitching and moaning. She was bleeding, though, from what looked like both ends.

"Dear God," James whispered. "You don't mean..."

The creatures both let out what James could only assume was a chuckle of their own, as one of them positioned itself in front of him while the other went to his rear. He felt his pants being ripped from his body, kicking his legs as best he could to fight it.

"All right, fellas. It's time to have some fun!" RJ yelled out.

James looked over to RJ and watched as he began to stroke the smallest penis James had ever seen. It couldn't have been any larger than the length from the tip of his pinky finger to the first knuckle, and it was the only thing he'd seen in real life that would fit the definition of a legitimate micropenis. For a brief second, James felt a sense of sadness and shame for RJ as he thought back to the comment he'd made earlier about how his friends call him *Big Daddy*. If that truly was the case, James thought, it was a drastic overstatement.

"Okay, let 'em rip! Bid Daddy says so!"

The last thing James saw was a gargantuan bigfoot penis being forced into his mouth before his eyes were swamped in the creature's pubes. As he gagged and choked, fighting for precious oxygen, he felt the other hairy hands of the true big daddy of the woods grip his hips as the other beast inserted itself deep into his rectum.

In front of them, RJ stroked his micropenis with two fingers, legs splayed over the arms of the chair as he pinched a nipple between forefinger and thumb. "That's it," he moaned. "Big Daddy does the fuckin' 'round 'ese woods."

TROUBLE DOLLS

IEGO WAITED INSIDE THE ROOM UNTIL THE LAST possible minute. He didn't want to be seen, especially by *him*. The second bell rang and everyone dispersed, funneling into classrooms left and right. He had exactly one minute to get from his homeroom to Mr. Harper's class at the other end of the hall, and every second counted. He stuck his head outside the door and looked both ways. The coast was clear, so he bolted.

He bobbed and weaved between the stragglers like a prized fighter slipping the jab. The rubber on the bottom of his sneakers gripped the floor and made a squeaking sound as he rounded the corner, and there, just across the hall, he saw Mr. Harper's room. He glanced at the clock on the wall – thirty more seconds.

"I'm gonna make it," he whispered. "I'm gonna ma—"

Smack!

His vision went dark as his face slammed into something hard, a force that sent him crashing to the floor. A deep thud echoed throughout the hall as his head bounced off the tile.

"Wh...what the—" he mumbled, shaking his head, an attempt at clearing the confusion.

"Run into somethin', asswipe?"

"Shut up, Rocky," he said, and tried to stand. "Why don't you just leave me alone?"

Placing his foot against Diego's chest, Rocky shoved him

back to the floor. "That's what you look like. You know that, right? A fuckin' asswipe. Like somebody shit all over you and rubbed it on your skin."

"If you don't stop I'll scream. I swear to God I'll scream, Rocky. You'll get suspended. Remember what Principal Hall said?"

"I don't give a shit about Principal Hall," Rocky said, kicking Diego again. "Why don't you just go back to Africa where you fuckin' came from?"

Through all the pain, Diego couldn't help but chuckle. "Shows what you know you fuckin' moron. I'm Mexican, not African." In a quick burst of energy, Diego scrambled to his feet.

"Why, you little son-of-a bitch!"

Diego took two steps backward and turned to run, but Rocky grabbed his backpack and threw him back to the floor. "What'd you say?" He kicked him again, harder this time. "Mexico's even worse than Africa. At least a fuckin' nigger knows when to keep their goddamn mouth shut."

Diego grunted and heaved as Rocky's foot sunk into his stomach, all the air forced from his lungs. "Just...leave me... alone," he managed, as he struggled to get his breath.

"That's what I thought, fuckin' browntard." Rocky spat in his face and turned to walk away. "Ain't no room for your kind around here. Remember that next time."

Diego lay sprawled out on the floor. His head throbbed, his heart hurt, and worst of all, he knew that being late again would get him suspended, too. There was no choice. He stood up, wiped the tears from his face, and walked into the office. "I need to see Mr. Hall."

"What's this about?" the secretary said, glancing up at him. When she saw Diego standing there, the side of his face already beginning to swell, she didn't need any more information. "Oh. You again. Have a seat, Diego. Mr. Hall will see you shortly."

§

Diego's mother sat in the principal's office tapping her foot, furiously. She was angry as the thought of her only son being bullied relentlessly stewed in her mind. "Look, I'm not sure what you want me to say," she said, defending Diego's actions. "My son was the victim, here. Just like all the other times."

"Mrs. Torres, please," Principal Hall said, his voice steady and low. "We do our best to prevent any—"

"Do your best? This is the *fifth* time in two months he's gotten into it with this little maniac. Are you going to sit there and tell me that this is the best you can do? What about the other kid? I want to know what kind of punishment he's getting for this."

"He'll be suspended as well, Mrs. Torres. We don't tolerate this kind of behavior here. Now, please—"

"Then it needs to stop, and it needs to stop right now!"

He chuckled under breath, the sound accompanied by a slight grin. "Well—"

"You're laughing? My boy's getting beat by this lunatic and all you can do is laugh?"

"Mrs. Torres, try to see it from our perspective. There's always two sides to every story." He reared back in his chair and sighed. "Diego, you," he hesitated, thinking delicately about his next statement. "Well, for lack of a better term, you're different. People around here, they just don't take to that kind of thing right away, you get my drift? Just look around. I don't mean to be disrespectful, but he's the only person of any color at this school. It's gonna take some time. Now, maybe Diego would be better off if he, I don't know, were to transfer?"

"Why you inconsiderate little motherfucking prick!" she yelled, scowling. "I'm sick of this. I'm sick and tired of being treated differently just because we're not white! How dare you tell me that I need to take Diego to another school. I'll have your job for this."

"Mrs. Torres, calm down. You're making this much bigger than it needs to be. Children fight. Especially—" he caught himself, his eyes widening as he glanced at Mrs. Torres. "Well, you know what I mean."

"Especially *what*, Mr. Hall? Mexicans? Brown children?"

"Now you're just putting words in my mouth."

"I know exactly what you meant. I know what you say to my son, the way he's treated." She stared into his eyes, unflinching, and took a deep breath. "Listen, Mr. Hall. Diego will stay home for three days. That's the length of his punishment, as unjust as it is. But when he comes back, you'll be lucky to have a job. This is racism, plain and simple." She slammed her hand down on the desk, the impact sending coffee springing from his mug. "And that boy will be lucky if he's not in juvenile detention...or worse!" She grabbed Diego by the arm and stormed out. "Come on, Diego. This will be made right, mark my words."

"Wow," the secretary said. "What was that all about? She sounds angry."

"Goddamn loudmouthed Mexicans," Principal Hall grumbled, as he walked to the doorway and watched them exit the building. "They think they deserve everything."

§

Diego was in his room lying in bed when he heard his mother calling for him.

"Diego! Diego, where are you?"

"In my room, Mom." He heard footsteps on the stairs and rolled to his side to greet her as she came up. "Do I have to go back tomorrow? I really don't like that place."

She stood in his doorway, hands behind her back. "Yes. You have to go back. We're a proud people, Diego. You have to show them that we will not stand for this type of ignorance."

"But Mom," he whined, burying his head in the sheets.

"It'll be fine, Diego. I'm going to go have another talk with Principal Hall tomorrow."

He looked back to his mom, his eyes growing dim. "Oh... when's Dad coming home?"

"I'm sorry, Diego. He won't be home for a few more days." She stepped into his room and sat next to him on the bed. "You know, he works so much because he loves you, right? That's the reason we moved here. To give you a better life."

"Yeah? A lot of good that did. I get the crap kicked out of me on a regular basis here. Back home I may not have gotten a good education, but I had friends and I was safe."

She moved her hands from behind her back revealing a large envelope. "Well, maybe this will help. Papa sent you something."

"Oh. What is it?"

"Well, I told him about your troubles and he wanted to help. It may not look like much, but when we were children, Papa would give them to us every time we had a problem.

Here, open it."

He tore open the envelope and dumped the contents on the bed. "What is this?" A small cloth bag no larger than his palm fell onto the sheets. "Looks like somebody lost an old sock."

"Go ahead," his mother encouraged, "look inside."

He loosened the string and turned it upside down. Five small dolls, each roughly half an inch tall, fell out. He took one in his hand and examined it. "Oh, great. Little stick dolls with painted on faces. A lot of help this will be. Does Papa think I'm a little girl or something?" He rolled his eyes and tossed the doll aside.

"Most people call them worry dolls, but some call them trouble dolls. That's what Papa always said they were."

"Yeah? Well if Rocky sees me with them, they'll definitely make trouble."

"I wouldn't be so sure, Diego," she said. "Aren't you even curious about how they work?"

He looked to his mother, knowing what she meant when asking something like that. She wanted him to ask the same question she'd just asked him. It was a classic case of reverse psychology for parents and kids.

"Fine, Mom. How are they supposed to help?"

"Thank you for asking," she said, smiling. "When we were children, Papa would give us dolls like this every time we were worried or troubled. Legend says, if you tell the dolls what you're worried about before putting them under your pillow at night, the worries will be gone the next morning, along with the dolls."

He hung his head and sighed. "I see. So, it's not something

that will *really* help, then. Just Papa and his silly magic."

"It's not technically magic, Diego. It's more like tradition. Papa is very traditional, you know that. You should give it a try." She picked up the envelope and walked toward the door. "You know, Papa told me that these are special dolls. He told me he blessed them himself."

"Okay, Mom," Diego replied. "But I'll bet I still get pummeled by Rocky again this week."

"Just try, okay?" She flipped the lights off. "I love you, Diego. Get some rest. They'll help. I promise."

He picked the dolls up and looked at them. "So, I'm supposed to tell one of you my worries, huh? Well, I'm gonna tell all five of you every single worry I have, cause they're big." He felt stupid for doing it, but he told them anyway. What did he have to lose? "I'm worried about being beat up by Rocky again tomorrow. I hate that kid. I'm worried that Principal Hall will just blame me for it, too. He hates me. I think it's because I'm Mexican. If you little guys really can take these worries from me, I'll owe you one." He laughed and put them in the bag, then slid it under his pillow. "But just like the tooth fairy, my guess is Mom will take you while I sleep."

§

"Now listen, Rocky. I called you in here this morning because I wanted to make sure things went a little more smoothly from here on out. I'm sorry I had to suspend you, but you were a little hard on him this time."

"You call that hard?" Rocky said, laughing. "I went easy on that little brown shit."

"Well, you need to ease it up a little more," replied Principal Hall.

"But you're the one who told me to do it!"

He smiled, gesturing with his hand. "I'm not sayin' to stop. Just don't be as rough. Let him know he doesn't belong here, but hit him in the stomach, the sides. You know, places that won't actually leave marks and bruises. That's the secret."

"Ha! I see. Yeah, I can do that. But, what about his mom? She was pretty mad. Think she'll go as far as gettin' you fired? Gettin' me put in—"

That brown bitch won't do a goddamn thing. Eventually she'll get tired of it and," he stopped. Something had caught his attention. He looked down to the space beneath his desk.

"And what?"

"Wait a minute," he said, staring at the space. "What's that?" He rolled his chair back and looked under the desk. There was something there, and whatever it was, it looked small, and it appeared to be moving. "Is it some kind of bug? Little fucker. I hate bugs."

Rocky leaned over the desk to see for himself. "You been playin' with dolls, Principal Hall?"

He squeezed his eyes together and took another look. "I-it does look like some kind of doll, huh? Bu—"

"Ouch! What the fuck!" Rocky grabbed the back of his neck, interrupting Principal Hall. Something had pinched or bit him. He grasped at it and threw it across the room. "Jesus! Somethin' got me good." Blood trickled around his neck and onto his collar bone. He walked over to see what it was that had got him, and when he realized, sheer confusion took hold. "I...it's another one of them dolls. What the fuck?"

"Agh!"

Rocky turned to see Mr. Hall digging at his ear wildly.

"What? What's wrong?"

"My ear! My fuckin' ear!"

"What *about* your ear?"

"The fuckin' doll! I...it hurts, it's in my ear!"

Rocky staggered back, his feet sliding across the floor until he bumped into the wall. "It can't be." There were two more of them, one hanging onto Mr. Hall's left sleeve, the other making its way toward his nostril, using the hairs of his mustache as a hold.

"They're alive!" Rocky yelped and bolted toward the door. Out of nowhere, a sharp pain pierced his right ear. "Fuck!" The pain intensified and a loud popping sound inside his head sent him pummeling to the floor. Before he had time to think, he saw one of them hopping toward his face. In its arms, it carried a pencil. "No!" The doll rammed it into his eyeball, piercing it with ease.

With one final push the doll drove the sharp point deeper into his skull, piercing his brain and leaving a heap of quivering flesh on the floor.

"Help! They're killing me!" Principal Hall fell, slamming the side of his face against the desk. He staggered to his knees and crawled toward Rocky's lifeless body. As he moved, the feeling of the dolls shifting in his ear canals was too much for him to handle. In an instant, the fifth doll wedged up into his nose. The feeling of cartilage and bone crunching as they chewed and gnawed their way into his brain was unbearable. Blood oozed from each orifice until, with one final, effortless cry, he collapsed on top of Rocky.

§

Diego and his mother drove into the schools parking lot, and to Diego's surprise, police cars and ambulances lined the drive just outside the front entrance.

"What in the world?" Diego said. "What happened?"

"I don't know. But if I had to guess, you won't be going to school today," his mother replied, a sort of cheerful glee in her voice.

They pulled up to a policeman who was talking to each driver in the line as he turned them away.

"Sorry, guys. No school today."

"What happened?" his mother asked.

"Not sure just yet, but looks like the principal may have gotten into a fight with a student." He turned to the entrance and back to Diego's mother. "Pretty rough in there."

"Oh dear. Anyone hurt?"

With a nod of his cap, the policeman politely turned them away. "Sorry ma'am, I'm not at liberty to say. Turn on around and head back, now. We still got a lot of work to do."

Diego stared behind him, his mind going crazy with thoughts of who, what, and why. They cleared the vehicles and got to the intersection of the schools drive and the main road. He turned back to look again and he saw two men carrying someone out on a stretcher. He couldn't be sure, but he *thought* one might've been Rocky. Diego sat in silence the whole car ride home.

As they turned into the driveway of their home, his mother looked over at him and smiled, a look of ease in her eyes. It was a mischievous sort of smile, like she knew for certain what had happened, but didn't want to share it just yet. "It'll be okay, Diego," she said, breaking the silence. "Everything will be okay now."

He looked at his mother as he stepped out of the car. "Huh?"

"Still think Papa's crazy?" she said, winking at him.

"What do you mean?"

"Well, you won't have to *worry* about either of your *troubles* anymore, right? I mean, I'm guessing that's what you told them."

"The dolls?" He dropped his backpack in the grass and ran upstairs. He rushed into his room and drove his arm under the pillow. "Whew!" He took a deep, relieving breath. "For a minute there, I actually thou—"

As he pulled the bag out, he noticed that it was wet. He held it up in front of himself and studied it closely. It was spotted with a thick crimson substance that was sticky to the touch. He dropped it on his bed and began to shake uncontrollably.

"What's wrong, Diego?" his mother whispered from the doorway behind him. "They took your troubles away, didn't they?"

A COLLECTION OF SOULS

THE HOUSE SAT LOW IN THE VALLEY, ITS POSITION BETWEEN the mountains nearly concealing it from William's sight. It seemed to be waiting for him, a refuge from the bitter arctic cold. He looked around, tried to trace his path, but the snow seemed to be falling endlessly. It came with such ferocity that footsteps made only seconds before had already been obliterated.

"Holy shit, a house! A fucking house!" he cried. As he pushed through the snow toward the structure, his gaze fell on an angry purple sky in the distance.

The storm was just beginning.

Thorns ripped his jacket, scratched his face like a wild animal as he pushed through overgrown shrubs and briar thickets, all the while trying to keep his attitude positive. He'd seen enough survival shows to know that once you lose that, everything goes south fast.

Someone will help me...they have to. I can't die out here, not like this. I've gotta get back.

The windows were glazed in a milky white film and creeper vines grew from a cracked foundation; all signs that suggested it was vacant. If not for a string of white smoke rising from the chimney, a sight that had been obscured from a distance by the onset of snow, he would have lost all hope. Instead, the smell of the burning wood settled his twisting stomach and brought a sense of ease.

On the front porch, William pressed his face against a window and rubbed the glass with his coat sleeve. "Hello, is anyone there?" A fire roared in the fireplace and candles did a poor job of lighting the rest of the space. "Is there anyone home? Please, I...I'll freeze to death." His left thumb massaged his ring finger, thoughts of his wife and baby girl filled his mind.

"I should've never come up here alone," he whispered. He peered in the window again, hopeful, and this time there was movement. "Hey, please," he yelled. "I...I need help, shelter!"

He ran across the porch to a second, less obscured window and squinting, straining his vision as if that would somehow break through the stain. A small doorway came into focus. Just beyond, a dirty kitchen spilled a piss yellow light into the hall.

"Please, is anyone there?"

Across the floor, a cloud of dust stirred, forming a trail as a small body scurried closer. A little voice, low in volume but high in pitch, broke the silence. "What? Who's there? It's not time yet. I need more time!"

His face pressed against the glass, William saw what appeared to be a small woman. "Please, ma'am, I need shelter," he begged, moving his head from side to side. "I was out hiking and this storm blew in out of nowhere." His hands found his face, and he exhaled warm air into his fists. "I...I got lost. If I don't find someplace to take shelter, I'll freeze to death."

She shuffled from one foot to the other, skeptical of William's intentions. "This place is a good piece from any house or road. You gotta be tryin' pretty damn hard to get lost out here, son."

"Please, ma'am, can I come in?"

Her eyes scrunched together as she studied him. "I know better than that. Ain't no reason to be hikin' all the way out here. What's your name?"

He rubbed his arms to generate precious warmth, but little more than a dull pressure could be felt. "William, ma'am, my n-n-name is W-William B-B-Blanton. I was c-c-camping, and—" His body shivered, forcing a brief pause. "I-I'm freezing-g-g. P-p-please?"

The old woman scooted closer to the window and looked up at him. She saw that ice had formed at the base of his nostrils and she shook her head. "Don't you lie to me, son. You tell me the truth." Her lips curled, revealing yellow teeth stained with age. "I just might be the only thing between you and the coffin tonight, so you better damn well be honest with me. Did *He* send you?"

"N-no, m-m-ma'am. N-nobody sent m-me. I'm t-t-telling you. I was c-c-camping and—"

She watched his hands quiver, his skin turning from shades of light pink to pale blue as he stuttered. "Forgive me, son. I'm just a little cautious," she said, gesturing toward the door. "Now, because I'm a good person, I'll let you stay, but only tonight. Then you're on your own. Understand?"

The cold gripped his lips like icy fingers, pinching down on them until the words moved faster than his mouth would allow. "Th-th-thank you, m-ma'am."

§

The warmth from the fire brought feeling back to William's fingers and toes. He stared into the flames as they danced back and forth, every sway appearing intentional, as if the fire itself was alive and trying to mesmerize him. To his side, he caught a glimpse the old woman watching.

"I'm sorry, ma'am. It's just that this fire's warming me up and making me a bit tired. I didn't mean to be rude. What did you say your name was?"

"I didn't," she replied, abruptly. "*Ma'am* will do just fine." She watched him closely; each move he made carefully monitored as if she thought of him as some sort of alien threat. "You sure you ain't fibbin' to me, boy?"

He turned to the old woman, a confused look on his face. "Ma'am?"

"You're an awfully big feller and I don't recognize you. You say you ain't from around 'ese parts. Hard to trust people like you, if you know what I mean. Especially with me livin' out here all alone since my husband's passing." She looked at him with confidence, her eyes roaming up and down as if to size him up. "He sends a few every year, but I need a little more time, you see? It's been a little...well, slow."

"Oh...yeah?" William replied, confused.

"He sends them for my collection."

Silence found them both. It was the sort of quiet that seems to stun your hearing more than the loudest noise.

"Uh, I'm not sure I follow, ma'am."

She snorted and rolled her beady little eyes. "Don't you give me that nonsense! You know damn well who *He* is, don't you, boy?"

"I'm afraid you've lost me. I don't know who or what it is that you're talking about."

She took a step back and looked at William. "I ain't sure about you just yet, boy. It's been a while, but the time just ain't exactly…" She hesitated, thinking carefully about her next words. "Well, never mind all that. It's close, and that'll have to be good enough. I'll have what I need soon."

He ran his fingers through his hair, wiping away the accumulated sweat and melted snow and rubbing his palms against his pants. "Umm, okay?"

"My husband used to keep me company." She sighed; her gaze fixed on the floor. "He would help with my collectibles. You know, help to keep them neat and organized. Since his passing, well, it's gotten a bit messy."

Unsure of what to say, William thought about what it must be like to be all alone and live in such a remote area. He looked at his wedding ring again and frowned. "I'm sorry for your loss, ma'am. Losing a loved one is always tough. I wouldn't even want to imagine losing my—"

"Oh, it ain't easy," she interrupted. "When they get out of order, *He* most certainly doesn't like it."

"Oh. I see. I'm sorry, ma'am, but would you mind if I asked, *who* doesn't like it?"

She peered over at William with a curious, almost dumbfounded look in her eyes. "You mean, you really don't know? You don't know who *He* is?"

"Well…no. I've no idea what you're talking about. I told you, I was just camping and got lost. These trails out here, it's like they move around. There one minute, no sign of them the next. It was very strange."

She circled to his side, placed a hand on his shoulder. "Yes, it most certainly can be. This place can get a little weird at times, I suppose."

"So, is he a friend, this man you keep referring to?"

Her eyes narrowed to thin slits as she clenched her frail, thin fists. "Not quite. *He* is the one who wants my collection. *He* is the one who walks in darkness."

"The one who walks in darkness? Like, a park ranger or something?"

The old woman chuckled. It was almost as if she were relieved at William's apparent blind ignorance. "Somethin' like that, yeah."

William sat in silence and tried not to make direct eye contact with the old woman. Thoughts were running through his mind, thoughts that she just might be a little on the crazy side. Or perhaps she was just old and confused. Lonely, maybe. Whatever it was really didn't matter to him at this particular moment, though. He was alive, and he was warm.

"Well, it sounds like you've got a fine collection, I suppose," he said, trying to make conversation. "Oh, and I meant to ask, you wouldn't happen to have a phone? I'd like to call my wife and daughter to let them know I'm okay."

"*Daughter*?" the old lady replied, an interest that bordered the lines of creepy showing in her voice. "Why, you didn't mention you had a daughter." She walked around the room as a new energy seemed to overtake her.

William chuckled nervously. "Yes, ma'am. Sarah is her name. She's six years old. I'd like to le—"

"He just *loves* children," she whispered under breath. "This *is* a special day."

"Uhm, excuse me?"

"Oh. Uhm, m...my husband. He loved children," she said, pausing to think. "I'm sorry. There's no phone out here. We're all alone."

"Oh," he said with a sigh, staring down at his wedding ring. "Kinda figured. Well, maybe I'll just try to get some rest then. Get a good early start tomorrow. You do know the way back to Black Mountain?"

"Oh, absolutely."

"Great. Uh, where could I sleep?"

"Yes! Sleep. That would be best for you." She scuttled across the room to an old sofa, slapping it as if inviting a dog up. "Here. You can sleep right here."

Dust rose from the cushions and filled the air, forcing William to cough. "Okay. That's fine. Again, I just wanted to say that I appre—"

"Just one thing, though," she said, interrupting him. "Whatever you need, have at it. There's not much food in the kitchen, but take what you want. The door under the stairs, though," she pointed, "that door stays locked for a reason. I wouldn't want you gettin' hurt. Understand? Under absolutely no circumstance are you to open that door."

"Oh, absolutely, ma'am. Under no circumstances am I to open that door. Got it."

§

William had just drifted off to sleep when the noises started. They were quiet at first, and hard to distinguish from the wind. He tried ignoring them, but they grew louder with each passing minute until they finally forced his attention.

"Whatnaworlisat?" he mumbled. He jerked his head from the cushion and a glob of snot stretched between it and his face. He listened for a moment, still half asleep, but when nothing happened, he put his head back down. Just as he'd convinced himself that the noises were all in his head, nothing but a semi-dream state, they returned, only louder this time.

Mumbles, words, voices.

"What the hell?"

They were faint, but they were there, and they were coming from somewhere down the hall.

He raised his head and looked, but the room was dark, only a dull glow from the fire remained. On tiptoe, he crept across the floor. With each step, the sounds became clearer, more audible. When he reached the hall, he cupped his hand behind his ear and moved his head from side to side, trying to pinpoint their source.

"They're coming from under the stairs," he whispered. "Is that," he listened closely, holding his breath so that no other sounds could distort it. "It...it is? It sounds like, like people." Confused, he stared down the hall. His mind wouldn't let him believe what he heard, but there was no other explanation. He was hearing whispers. He was hearing *people*.

Their volume increased as if whoever was making the noise could hear him on the other side of the door.

The sounds were clear. Hundreds, thousands of whispers. Men, women, children.

"Help us. Set us free," one of them said.

"I want to go home," another begged. "Please? I miss my daddy."

Every voice unique, every plea different, each one relaying the same final message - *help us.*

Adrenaline surged through his veins; his heart beat a tattoo in his chest as his mind filled with crazy thoughts. *She has children down there. She collects humans. She's a fucking lunatic!* He thought of his own daughter and his heart dropped to his stomach. *She was asking about Sarah! I've got to help them.*

"Hold on," he yelled, thinking of nothing other than freeing the old lady's prisoners. "I'll get you out." He grabbed the knob and giggled. "It's locked." He drove his foot into the door, but it wouldn't budge. "Just, just hang on. I won't lea—" He froze. Just above him was a familiar scurrying sound slithering across the floor upstairs. "She's coming. I have to think of something. Don't worry, I won't leave you. I just need to...I've got it!" He ran down the hall and grabbed the poker from the fireplace. "This should do the trick."

William knew that the end was near; that he had to get them out before the old lady came downstairs. Sure, he was much larger than her, but if she was holding people captive, she would almost certainly have a gun, and when you're shot in the head, it doesn't matter how big or how strong you are.

He pried the padlocks off the door, only the deadbolt remained. "Everyone stand back! I'm kicking it in!" Placing several feet between himself and the room, he ran toward the door, slamming into it shoulder first. As it gave way, he yelled, "come on, hurry! She's coming!"

He looked around the room, ready to help the captives, but there was no one there. A dry sensation found his tongue, as if his mouth had suddenly filled with cotton. Although the room was empty, the noises were louder than ever. He looked in every direction, yet nothing was there except for a row of dust covered shelves on the back wall that was filled with mason jars.

"Where are you? Is there some kind of trapdoor or a secret room?" His hands trembled with confusion, with fear.

The voices continued.

"Help us!" a child cried.

"Please, set us free!" yelled another.

A small movement on one of the shelves caught his attention. "What the hell is that?" As he made his way toward it, he noticed that each jar was filled with greenish-gray smoke that swirled around as if it were alive and trying to escape. Some were brighter than others, but each one appeared to be moving on its own. "I...it *can't* be," he said, watching the jars. "Is it...coming from the jars?" He wiped away a thick layer of dust from the first one he grabbed.

A label read, *J. Jude - 1901.*

What is this?

He reached for another. *A. Maynard - 1753.*

Another, *M. Harris - 1956.*

"This can't be happening to me. This can't be *real.*"

Behind him, a loud scream erupted, piercing his eardrums. "I knew it! I knew *He* sent you, boy!"

William turned to find the woman standing in the doorway. The jar slipped from his hands, shattering against the hard floor on impact.

"My collectibles!"

The contents swirled around in the air as it rose toward the ceiling. "Thank you," it whispered, and in one impressive bright green surge, it disappeared.

"What *was* that thing?"

The old woman shriveled her nose and scrunched her brow. "Look at what you've done. You've set one free," she cried, as her eyes turned to pitch black.

William stumbled backward. "Set what free?"

"You know what they are. Don't play stupid, not with me. He sent you here to steal my collection, like he does with all of them." She motioned to the remaining jars. "He sent you here to steal my souls, didn't he? You're his collector!" She started toward William, ready to protect what was hers.

"Souls? You...you're crazy!" In an attempt to get away from her, his back bumped against the shelf, shaking it.

The old woman licked her lips hungrily. "You set one free. Now I've got to find another to take its place." She raised her hand, her fingertips replaced with long, jagged claws. "Come here, boy."

"This can't be happening. I...I'm hallucinating. It can't be real. It's all some kind of really fucked up nightmare!"

"Oh, it's real. You're about to feel just how real it is for yourself. I won't give you to him, though. I'll keep you locked in a jar for as long as I can."

"What are you talking about? Please, let me go!"

The old woman swiped her hand and her long claws sliced into his cheek, a hit that sent him falling to the floor. She grasped the back of his neck, her nails pressed firmly against his skin. "You think you can break something five hundred years strong? Do you really think you can break my pact with *Him*?" She stroked his cheek with the back of her forefinger. "That's my food. Only thing that keeps me livin', and you tried to take it from me."

He grabbed her wrist, but her strength was too much. "I...I don't want *anything*," William pleaded. "You're crazy. I don't know anything about any of this!"

"Oh, he sends people like you from time to time to collect his share. Problem is, I want 'em all." She tightened her grip, and a trickle of blood ran down his neck. "Let it go, boy. Just give it to me."

His body went limp as she held him in the air. Her tongue slid up his cheek, tasting his skin as she clenched his windpipe. "Yours is a strong one, boy. Here it comes. Open wide!"

His throat convulsed, his stomach churned, and something began to make its way up into his neck. His eyes grew darker, heavier.

"Yes," the old woman said.

Memories danced with the spots in his vision: Him holding Sarah as she learned how to ride her first bike; the day he brought home Roo, the family cat; that sweet smell of the shampoo Sarah used on those golden locks of hair.

I've gotta get outta here.

He flung his body wildly, hands flailing to his sides. His arm crashed into the top shelf knocking every jar to the floor.

"No! What have you done?" The old woman threw William to the side and scrambled for her precious souls. "My collectibles!"

William fumbled to his feet as he gasped for air and staggered toward the door, kicking her in the side as he passed.

She cried out in agony and reached for his ankle. "Come back here! I'm not done with you!"

He slammed into the ground face first. As he glanced back, he saw a dark cloud forming in the room. The souls, thousands of them, circled above her head.

"I'll kill you, boy. You and your famil—"

One by one, they flew into her mouth. The souls forced their way down her gullet and into her stomach. She gripped her throat with both hands, trying to fight it, but nothing could stop the hordes of souls as they filed in. With each poof of smoke that slid into her body, she grew larger.

"Holy shit!" William jumped to his feet and ran toward the door.

The old woman's body swelled to twice its normal size. "You'll pay, boy," she screamed. "You'll pay!"

He rounded the corner of the main room just as a loud, powerful explosion echoed from the space under the stairs.

§

William woke to someone knocking at the door. Unsure of where he was, he opened his eyes slowly, trying to get his bearings.

"Wh-what happened? Where am I?"

Knock, knock, knock.

He shook his head to try to shake the remaining cobwebs. "Wha...I, I don't know where I am." Around him lay the pieces of the old woman. Her blood splattered against the walls, bits of flesh and bone scattered on the floor; the rancid smell of spilled guts clinging to his nostrils.

"M-m-" He heaved, and the contents of his belly spewed across the floor.

Knock, knock, knock.

He wiped his mouth, finally realizing where the sound was coming from. "Someone's at the...I-I'm saved!" He staggered to his feet and toward the door. "Please, help me," he cried, opening the door. "Can you please he—" William looked on, but the sight of the person in front of him seemed to paralyze his tongue.

"Why, hello there," a man said.

His clothes were torn and ragged, stained with blood and

dirt. A smile stretched across his face, the skin of his cheeks ripped to form a patchwork of holes, exposing bone. Maggots writhed from the open wounds, chewing on the dried, leathery tissue that remained. He held up his hand, and between his thumb and forefinger was a small glass vial.

"Y...you're—" William managed, noticing the label on the vial.

Blanton - 2017.

"Mr. Blanton, I believe?" A large worm slithered from the man's right eye and a long, snake-like tongue curled around it, dragging it into his mouth the way a child slurps up a spaghetti noodle. "I believe you have something that belongs to me, don't you?"

"You're...*Him.* You're the...the one who walks in darkness."

The man laughed, releasing a foul odor into the air. "On your knees, *boy*! Time for you to take your place."

Unable to control himself, William fell to the floor as the man commanded. His muscles were failing, he was no longer able to control his own body. "My daughter. She needs me," he said, as a tear rolled down his cheek.

The man used a long, pointed claw to wipe away the salty liquid, placing it on his own tongue. "Mmmmm." His eyes, a grayish green hazy color, rolled to the back of his head. "Her name is...*Sarah,* aged...six, I believe? That is correct, isn't it?"

His body frozen; William's eyes grew large. "How did you—"

"How perfect an age. So small. So tender and naïve. They have the purest of souls." A sinister grin engulfed the man's face as he inhaled deeply. "I'm going to enjoy this."

"But...my daughter! What about Sarah?" William whined.

"Oh, don't you worry about her, Mr. Blanton. She'll be my *special* collectible. You see, I've always wanted my very own daughter. I'll take *good* care of her for you."

THE FINAL SACRIFICE

JAMES HAD JUST FINISHED MAKING A DRINK WHEN HE SAW the next customer step up to the counter. "Damn," he said under breath, eyes widening as his mouth flopped open.

She smiled at him, short blond hair tucked neatly behind her ears. "Hey there. How's it goin'?"

Reflexively, he grinned. Embarrassment overwhelmed him as his cheeks flushed. He turned his head and took a deep breath. "Now that's exactly what I need," he whispered to himself. He grabbed a plastic lid and placed it on the coffee cup in his hand, then slid the drink to the end of the bar. "Large vanilla iced coffee for Ben," he called, hoping she wouldn't reach for it. He *definitely* didn't need someone named Ben coming to pay him a visit.

James turned back to the register and looked at her, trying to not make his feelings super obvious, which inevitably resulted in him coming off as awkward and nervous. He cleared his throat and wiped his palms on his apron while the girl shuffled her feet.

"Hey there," he finally managed. "What, uh...what can I get for you today?" He dropped his head slightly and glanced at her from the corner of his eye.

Head tilted down, she ran her fingers through her hair and bit her lower lip, sliding it gently from between her teeth.

"Sure. How about a mocha Frappuccino?"

James grinned. "Absolutely. What size?"

"Let's just do the smallest you have." She motioned to her waist and giggled. "I'm tryin' to watch my figure."

"Psh...whatever, girl. You definitely don't need to watch anything." He winked and wrote her drink order on the cup. "Mind if I ask your name?"

"My name, huh? A bit forward, don't you think? Must be awful sure of yourself..." She paused, her eyes moving up and down his body, eventually landing on his name tag. "James?"

His smile grew large and he placed both hands on the counter. "It's for the drink order."

"O...oh. Uhm, well then...it's Samantha. My name's Samantha."

They both laughed, a gesture that helped to ease the tension.

"Listen," James said, checking his watch. "My shift's over in about ten minutes. How about I make your drink and come out there with you for a bit? We could...I don't know...get to know each other, maybe?"

She shuffled a bit more, bit her lip again, flirting. "I mean, sure. That sounds good to me."

The positive reinforcement triggered an increase in his confidence. He'd been in this situation many times before, and he knew how to get the job done. Closing wasn't his problem. Though, even with his flawless success rate, each time the hunt began, the fear of failure made his nerves quiver.

"Yeah? Well then," he leaned in close, lowering his voice. "Maybe we could get outta here? Maybe go back to *my* place...I mean, *if* you're comfortable with that, or course."

She reached out and tugged lightly on his collar, her tongue slid across her upper lip. "Depending on how your conversation is, you just might be in luck."

He laughed. "I'll get right on this drink."

"Just meet me out on the patio when you're done. Take your time."

§

Samantha was skimming through the newest issue of the local newspaper when James placed her frappe next to her.

"So, *Samantha...*" he paused, cocking an eyebrow as he stood next to her. "I don't think I've seen you around here before."

She glanced up from the paper and slid her sunglasses down just enough that they weren't covering her eyes. "Well... *James*," Samantha replied, mimicking his actions. "It appears that in addition to being easy on the eyes, you're also quite observant."

"Yeah, I can be," he smirked, eyeing her up and down. "When I see something that really catches my attention, that is."

Her eyebrows raised. She lowered the paper all the way to the table.

"Or, someone..."

"Yeah, me too." She looked at his hand as he took a sip of his own coffee, her attention fully on a one of his many tattoos. "So, I gotta ask, what's with the tattoos? They look pretty unique."

He put the cup down on the table and extended both hands, spreading his fingers. On each digit, between the top two knuckles, was a small symbol, each one different. "Ah.

119

That's what attracted you to me, huh? You like a guy with tattoos."

She chuckled in a playful tone, then slid her foot against his leg, softly rubbing it. "That's not what attracted me to you, but they are a bit unusual, wouldn't you say? I don't know if it was the ink that got me, I just like a certain type of guy. A guy that's *different*, I suppose you could say."

"Mhm. I'm not like any guy you've ever met, that much I can guarantee. I'll warn you, though, before I go any further. That exact question has gotten quite a few girls in trouble," he said with a wink.

"Oh, I'm a big girl. I think I'll take my chances," Samantha said, grinning.

James nodded. "Okay. Don't say I didn't warn you."

"Never."

"Well, I guess you're curious what they mean, right? Most people are."

"That's a start, sure. I just think they're very interesting."

James chuckled. "I guess I can tell you...but the problem with that is, you wouldn't believe me if I did."

She cocked her head and squinted. "Really? Now you *know* that just makes me wanna hear it even more."

"Trust me, girl. Nobody *ever* believes me."

"Let me see." She moved closer, examining each one in detail. "They're all different, which suggests to me that they likely mean or represent something to you, maybe something *special*. And they look very professional. Extremely detailed. Better than any tattoo I've ever seen, in fact. That shows even more that you care what they look like. All that attention to detail."

"Hmm, is that so?"

"I mean, I'm just taking a shot in the dark, since you seem like you don't wanna tell me."

"Do go on, then. You have my interest."

Her foot moved further up his leg, working up to his inner thigh.

James shifted, his smile widening as his muscles began to relax.

"Now, again, keep in mind that I'm just guessing."

"Oh, of course. I totally understand."

"But I'm gonna say it's some kind of list, maybe? Things you want in life, or maybe things you've accomplished? Am I anywhere even remotely close?"

Their eyes met, intensity growing between them. Suddenly, as if scripted in a screenplay, they both burst out laughing.

"A list, huh? I guess it's something like that, actually." He scooted closer forcing her foot deeper into his groin. "Mmm."

She placed the frappe to her lips and slid her tongue around the straw in a very seductive fashion. "Then tell me, *James*. What do they mean? What is it that's so special to you?"

"Are you sure you wanna know? I mean absolutely, positively *sure*? Remember, I told you you're not gonna believe it, and in fact, I just might have to kill you once you know."

She drew a long sip of her drink. "Oh, I wanna know, James. I *really* wanna fucking know."

James laughed. "Okay then, here it goes. Better brace yourself."

She winked, her foot now massaging his cock as it began to engorge, filling with blood. "I'm fully braced."

James moaned quietly, eyes narrowed to tiny slits. "Mmmm. Well, Samantha...I'm sort of a serial killer."

Without reaction, Samantha looked into his eyes, never breaking concentration. "Oh yeah?"

"Yeah. Kind of, I guess."

"Hmm." She pushed harder into his now throbbing cock. "And what does *that* have to do with your tattoos?"

"You see, each symbol represents a specific death." He pointed to his right forefinger. "See this one? It's a pit of fire. It represents a woman I burned to death."

"Oooo. Scary." Samantha took another long sip of her drink, holding the straw between her tongue and teeth when she was finished.

"It was scary, actually. Very scary. Human flesh has a very distinct smell when it's melting. It's not a pleasant one. I could smell it as it melted away from her bones. She screamed the entire time."

"Damn," Samantha replied. "Sounds...*hot*. Get it?"

James cocked his eyebrow, surprised. "Nice one." He pointed to his left ring finger. "And this one is rain. It represents the woman I drowned."

"Interesting," she replied, finishing her drink. "How'd that one make you feel?"

"That one was tough to watch. I can't swim, and it made me imagine myself being drowned. I held her head below water while she thrashed and begged me to let go, but I couldn't. I had to hit her a couple times to get her to calm down. But she finally stopped."

Samantha grinned, a quiet chuckle escaping her mouth. "*Interesting.*"

James looked at her, her response a bit off. "Interesting? How so?"

"Well, it has a flaw when you think about it. I mean, if you're a serial killer, why do you leave the evidence on your skin? Wouldn't that be a good way to get caught?" She pushed harder into his cock, feeling it throb with every stroke of her foot.

"Oh. Well, I don't put them there. They just appear."

"Like magic, you mean?"

"Something like that," he said, with a chuckle. "I sold my soul to Satan so that I would be rich. This whole thing is kinda what I have to do for him as a payment for services rendered. Each of these tattoos is a way to mark me for that, I suppose. They just show up once I kill someone."

Samantha wiped her brow and began fanning herself with her hand. "Ah, I see. The age-old bargain. So, how do you determine who dies and how?"

"It's all in the contract I signed. Well, I mean...*how* they die is. He doesn't care *who* it is, just how. You see, I'm required to take the souls of ten women and feed them each to a specific demon. Once it's complete, Satan will honor our deal."

"Yeah, you were right."

James looked at her, confused. "Huh?"

"That *is* a story," she said with a laugh. "But i-it's not the b-best way to pick up w-w-women." She shook her head and continued to fan herself.

James laughed. "Are you okay? You look like you're getting a bit sick."

"I-I just feel a little woozy is all. It m-must be the heat g-getting to me."

James looked to her cup and grinned. "Yeah, the heat. That's all it is."

Her eyes widened, adrenaline coursed through her veins as the realization of what was happening hit her. "W-wait. Y-you drugged—"

He held up his right hand and pointed to his pinky finger. "You're gonna be number ten."

"B-but it can't be."

"Yeah...it can."

She looked to him; fear radiated from her eyes as her vision began to blur.

§

Samantha woke to the smell of something burning. She lifted her head slowly as she tried to see where she was. Around her was a circle of black candles, all of them lit.

"Where the hell am I?"

"Ah! Finally awake, are we?"

She turned her head and saw James standing just outside of the circle, hands behind his back.

"You were out for a while. I was beginning to think I wouldn't get my chance to have fun with you."

She raised to a seated position and attempted to stand, quickly realizing that her wrists and ankles were bound.

"Duct tape? Really? How cliché."

"Yeah, sorry about that. It's just that, based on past experiences, you know, numbers one through nine, if you don't restrain them, they tend to try and run. Then you gotta chase them down, end up hurting them more than they need to be hurt, all that shit. Makes a whole mess, really."

"I could see that." She glanced to her wrists again. "And I

can see you're a kinky one."

"Ha! You seem to be in good spirits. Kinda strange, actually. I'm sorry to say, though, that those good spirits are about to end. This is gonna end rather badly for you, baby. All these jokes won't help a bit." James pulled a knife from behind his back and watched the candle flames flicker over the steel blade.

"Oh! You mean...we're not gonna fuck?"

James burst out with laughter. "Seriously? You're still on that? Goddam, girl! You must really be horny for me, huh? I thought you'd have realized by now that you're gonna die! I mean, I drugged you and you just woke up bound in tape!"

Her eyes grew larger, mouth dropped open.

"Now, now, don't worry. You'll black out pretty fast. I'd imagine the pain will be too intense for you not to. You see, I gotta skin you. And you kinda gotta be alive for it." He bared his teeth and winced.

"B-b-but—"

"I'm still gonna fuck you, though. Don't you worry about that."

A grin stretched across her face and she began to chuckle.

James squinted his eyes and shook his head in confusion. "You think it's funny?"

Her chuckles turned into a full on cackle.

"What the..." James stepped closer to her. "You understand what's about to happen, right? I'm *going* to rape you, repeatedly, and then I'm *going* to skin you alive!"

She fell to her back, writhing on the floor as she continued to laugh uncontrollably.

"What? What's so goddamn funny?" James watched

her in disbelief. He couldn't imagine anyone thinking that their impending rape and murder was funny. "Y-you're not supposed to be laughing! I-I'm gonna rape you! I'm going to fucking slaughter you!"

The room suddenly fell silent. Samantha lay motionless on the floor in front of him, the only sounds James could hear were those of his own heart beating madly. He drew in a breath and held it, trying to steady himself.

Like crystal shattering in the night, a deep, raspy voice sliced the quiet in half.

"Do you recognize me now, boy?"

James stood, frozen in place as the sound of Samantha's new voice took hold of him. As he tried to comprehend what was happening, he watched her roll to her back and began to twitch.

"Answer me. I command you!" She yelled out.

James tried to speak, but the words just wouldn't come. He began to shake, the sound and tone of the commanding voice coming from Samantha's body becoming more and more familiar.

Still bound, she rose to her feet in one fluid motion. Her eyes rolled back showing only their whites, her head cocked to the side. "I knew if I took the form of a sweet and innocent girl you wouldn't be able to resist me. I see you've been busy."

The knife fell from his hands. "No...i-it's you?"

She smiled, the smell of rotten flesh exploding from her mouth as it filled the room. "I am Asmodeus, the seventh prince of Hell. I am the lord of lust. It is I with whom your deal was made, James. And it is I with whom it will *end*."

"A-A-Asmode—" he stuttered, falling to his knees. "I was

just about to give you your sacrifice! The final sacrifice to complete our—"

"Do you remember our terms?" the demon interrupted. "Do you remember the details in the contract that *you* signed with *your* own blood?"

"I-I was to bring you ten women. I was to kill them as instructed." He looked to the tattoos on his fingers. "Burn, Bleed, Hang, Drown—"

"Do not mock me, boy. I know the rules. I am the one who makes them!" Asmodeus commanded. "These sacrifices are not sufficient to appease me."

"Wh...what do you mean? I brought you nine women just as you asked." He pointed to the demon. "She, y...you were going to be number ten."

"You were to bring them to me cleaned. So that their sin would be *fresh*. These women were to serve as my slaves. To bring pleasure only to me."

"Clean? That wasn't part of the deal. How am I supposed to keep them clea—"

"They were tainted with your seed, boy! Each one came to me covered in the stench of human flesh and semen. *Your* stench! Your disgusting scent!"

"B-b-but, I didn't mean to—"

"You took liberties that you were not granted permission to take. For that, our deal is broken."

James stumbled backward on his hands, scooting across the floor like a cumbersome crab. "No. No! Th-that's not fair! I've done everything you asked!"

A deep laughter filled the room as Asmodeus levitated off the floor. His hands and feet broke free from the tape, arms extending to his sides. "There are consequences, boy." His mouth flung open wide, a series of pops and cracks as his head extended back, dislocating his jaw.

"Jesus," James whispered as tears began to drip down his cheeks. "Please help me."

One by one, he watched as a series of dark, human shaped hands clawed their way from the demon's mouth. Using his face as a springboard, each of them gripped around the edges of his mouth, and several bodies began to emerge.

"Th-this isn't real. It can't be happening."

Asmodeus's laughter continued as nine black, humanoid apparitions floated from within him, swirling like ink in water. In one loud crack, his jaw popped back into place and an evil smile covered his face. "Because the fate of these nine women has been lost to your sinful pleasure, you will now become *our* servant, for all eternity, *James*."

"No! No, this isn't fair! I did everything for you! Everything you asked of me!"

One by one, the apparitions shot into his body and lifted him into the air. He began to squirm in pain as they tore at his insides, pushing into his organs, ripping and scratching at his skin, leaving deep gashes from the inside out.

Asmodeus drew in a deep, satisfying breath and exhaled it slowly. "You will now be my personal servant of pleasure. *You* will serve as the final sacrifice."

Miss Molly, Miss Molly

"**G**ODDAMN!" SCOTT SAID, JUMPING AS A LOUD CRASH of thunder shook the whole house. "Now 'at sounds like a storm!" He looked at Janet, who was sitting next to him, threw his arm around her, and squeezed. He could tell she was bored and that maybe she didn't like the storm, but he was also hoping that both of those factors would aid in accomplishing his ultimate goal for the night. He slid against her and squeezed a little tighter. "Looks like we ain't goin' nowhere tonight, baby. Not until 'is storm passes, anyway."

"Oh boy," Janet sighed. "Maybe it'll be quick." She hoped so, anyway.

"Oh, now don't you go worryin' about the storm. I ain't gonna let nothin' git ya, girl. Trust me." His smile was bordering on 'creepy old man' status, but it didn't surprise anyone. His intentions were obvious. He was, after all, a *guy*.

Janet smiled back. "Oh yeah? What's gonna *git* me?"

"You never know, 'specially 'round 'ese parts. Whatever it is, though...you're safe as long as you stay right next to me."

Unphased by his poorly hidden perversion, she didn't seem to mind, pressing into him almost comfortably. Her boredom was evident, and, just like Scott and his perversion, she made no attempt at hiding it. She was from southern California, after all, and her Saturday nights typically involved more than just sitting in a house in the middle of nowhere with three people doing nothing during a thunderstorm. It wasn't really their fault, though, and she couldn't blame them. They were supposed to have gone to a movie tonight, but the impending storm put a damper on those plans fast. It could be worse, she knew, but it could also be better. She liked her new friends, at least. They shared lots of similar interests, and usually they had a good time together, but she was still getting used to the slower life of small-town Kentucky.

Add a stormy night on top of that and things got even slower, *real* fast. She'd never been a fan of thunderstorms in general, especially bad ones. There was just something about them, something about the feeling they brought on that sort of spooked her. It was almost as if she could feel the change in the energy associated with them, and unfortunately for her, this one was supposed to be a doozy.

The local weather folks had been calling for the possibility of severe weather for tonight since earlier in the week, and as it turns out, it appeared that they got this one right. Some of the more energetic meteorologic personalities had even gone as far as to say that tonight's storm could be the storm of a lifetime, something unlike anything most of their viewers had ever witnessed; a storm unlike anything Pine Grove had seen for the last hundred years, maybe longer.

"Oh, shut up Scott. You're not scarin' her. She's not a baby," Kris said, shaking her head at his stupid attempts.

Janet chuckled. "She's right. If you're trying to scare me, it's gonna take a little more than that. I'm not sure a storm will—"

Thunder rumbled in the distance; a loud crack popped almost directly overhead, spooking Janet.

Kris glanced at her, a wry grin covering her face. "Is that right? Could've fooled me."

She chuckled nervously, embarrassed at how it had got her. "Really. I'm not scared. Thunder just kinda puts me on edge a bit. Not used to it, and if I'm being honest, it kind of reminds me of gunshots."

"Oh, yeah. I guess I could see that. Kinda makes sense, comin' from the city and all." Kris paused, considering the difference in the environments in which they'd grown up. Southern California had a different reputation than eastern Kentucky, at least that was what she'd assumed based on all the rap songs and television shows she'd heard and seen. They shot guns here, too...but it just wasn't the same. "Well, whatever it is, it'll be fine. It's just a typical summer thunderstorm 'round here. Nothin' outta the ordinary."

"I don't know about gunshots, but I'm not a fan of thunderstorms either, especially when they get like this." Her hands rubbing her arms, Rachel walked over to the window to get a better look at what was happening. The sun had set more than an hour ago, yet it was still oddly bright. The western sky had taken on a dark shade of reddish purple, almost as if backlit by the sun. Large, thick clouds engulfed the mountains as they rolled through the sky from the head of Long Branch Holler. Her eyes widened; the mixing of colors almost hypnotizing as she gazed into the eerie darkness. It was almost as if she had to, almost as if she wasn't able to turn away.

She stared for a moment; the colors swirling together as strange dark splotches mixed with more vibrant hues to form odd shapes in the clouds. The way they moved made them look as though they were dancing for her, almost like they were alive and begging for her attention. If she looked hard enough, just enough out of focus, she was nearly able to convince herself that there was something there. Something that wasn't supposed to be. Figures forming in the clouds, arms and legs loosely materializing to wave at and taunt her. For a brief second, she was almost certain that something was looking down at her, something alive. And whatever that something was, it looked to be smiling.

What the...

Rachel shook her head and squeezed her eyes shut, turning away from the window.

No. No, it's not...

"Whoa, now, girl! You okay?"

Startled, Rachel opened her eyes to see Kris standing in front of her. "Oh! Y-yeah. I'm fine. I just...never mind. It's stupid. I was just looking at the storm."

Kris cocked her head. "You sure? You seem a little out of it."

Rachel looked back at the sky. "Yeah, I'm sure."

"It's supposed to be a pretty big one. The storm, I mean. They're sayin' it's gonna be bigger than anything we've ever seen around here. I know you don't like 'em, so I just figured I'd ask."

"I know." She faced her friend, a slight grin, eyes squinted, looking almost confused. "Hey, Kris...is it just me, or does it look kinda...I don't know...strange outside?"

"Strange?"

"Yeah, like...it's nighttime, but it's still bright enough to see. I wouldn't even need a flashlight to get around if I was out there. It looks like dusk or somethin', not the middle of the night."

Kris leaned over and looked for herself. "I mean, it's a *little* brighter, yeah. Maybe it's the moon backlightin' the clouds or somethin'. I don't know. I ain't no weather scientist."

"The moon?" Rachel raised an eyebrow, skeptical of the probability of her friend's suggestion. "*Maybe.* The clouds do look a little weird, too, so maybe that's all it is. It's almost like I could see somth..." She caught herself, not wanting to draw any more attention. She already didn't like storms. Both Kris and Scott knew this, but they also knew why she was particularly nervous about bad ones."

"Do what?" Kris said, studying her. "Rachel...you know 'at stuff ain't real. They're just stories."

She nodded anxiously; a bit ashamed that she let the stories get to her so badly. "I don't know. I just thought I saw somethin'. I know it's crazy."

Kris looked at the sky for herself. The colors of the sky were magnificent. There was no denying that. Something was certainly different about this particular storm. "I don't see anything. It looks wild out there for sure, but I don't see anything like...well...you know."

Rachel shuffled her feet, wanting to believe her friend. Wanting to believe that she was just being a stupid scaredy-cat that let too many tales sink into her gullible brain. It *was* almost idiocy, after all...what she'd thought she'd seen. It was all just an old story people told to scare little kids in town. "Yeah, I know. It's stupid, but I just thought..." She trailed off, her imagination wandering.

"You thought what?"

Rachel shook her head and forced a smile. "You know

what? You're right. It's nothing." She laughed it off, or tried to, anyway, until Scott caught wind of their conversation.

"Y'all ain't talkin' 'bout what I think you're talkin' 'bout, are ya?" He stood up, looking at them from across the room, a big dumb and cocky expression. "It might not be so crazy. What you *think* you saw out there, I mean."

Rachel and Kris turned around, giving him their attention. "Scott, stop it. She didn't say that. Hell, she wasn't even talkin' to you. Mind your own goddamn business for once, would ya?"

"Oh, come on now. Don't be a couple of babies. Besides, Janet ain't never heard 'bout her." He shot her a look, eyebrows raised. "I don't think...have ya?"

"No," Rachel started. "I didn't say a word, Scott. I was just sayin' it looked a little..." She took a quick look back at the sky. The air was still bright and colorful, but the swirling was gone. Just ominous and dark clouds pushing their way over the mountains and toward them. It was just a storm. Nothing more, nothing less. "It just looked a little weird, that's all." Her face was flushed now, slightly embarrassed.

"You *sure* that's all you was thinkin'?" he taunted.

"Yes. That's all. That stuff ain't real, anyway. Even if it *was* what I was thinkin'."

"Wait, what? Who haven't I heard of? What's not real?" Janet stood up and put her arm around Scott. "What are you all talking about?" She smiled, genuinely curious. It was obvious that the three of them knew something she didn't, which didn't surprise her. She'd only moved to Pine Grove six months ago, and the rest of them had been born and raised there. Even though it was a small as shit town, she hadn't had time to learn all the ins and outs of it, what to really say and not to say, or any of the local stories.

Scott grinned. "*Yeah*! *That's* what we can do! *Hell* yeah! I don't know why I didn't think of it earlier!" He had a crazed look in his eyes, a mixture of arrogance and, oddly enough, horniness. Why not, though? They couldn't go anywhere, at least until the storm passed, and who the hell knew how long that would be? His girlfriend was bored out of her mind, that was obvious as fuck, and if he wanted any shot at finally getting in her pants, which was supposed to have been happening after the movie they now couldn't make it to, this was a prime opportunity to do it. It was one of the oldest tricks in the book. *Scare* her into bed! "Yeah, and this is the *perfect* night to do it, too!"

"Do *what*?" Janet said, eager to hear. "What am I missing?"

Kris looked at Rachel, eyebrows raised as she shrugged. She knew it wasn't going to set well with her friend, but if she were being honest with herself, it was better than doing nothing. She was bored, too.

Rachel, on the other hand, was anything but amused. She rolled her eyes, shook her head in dispute. It wasn't real, none of it was...it *couldn't* be. But there was always the question of *what if*?

"I'm up for it," Kris said, mouthing the words 'I'm sorry' to Rachel, hoping she wouldn't be too mad at her.

"Great," Scott announced.

"Up for *what*?" Janet said. "What are you guys talking about? Somebody tell me!"

"It's a game. Something folks around here play now and then when they're feelin' particularly brave."

"Oooo, that sounds fun! What kind? Like a drinking

game?"

He shook his head slowly, attempting to build tension. "Nah, it ain't no drinkin' game. It's a scary one, and it's based on a story from around here. An old folktale, you might say."

"Oh. Interesting. Well, I'm bored out of my mind, so I'm definitely up for playing."

They all looked at Rachel. She tried to ignore them, staring at the ground. They could tell she was nervous, but in Scott's eyes, that made it all the more fun, and, more importantly to him, it made it easier to jump scare her at the end.

"Well," Kris said. "How about it, Rachel? You down?"

She shuffled her feet a bit and looked up her friends. "I...I don't know, guys. Y'all know how I feel about it and what they say about her. Especially during a thun—"

A rumble of thunder echoed in the distance and a sudden gust of wind rustled the dying October leaves.

Rachel jumped, her attention flinging to the window.

"Come on," Kris said. "It'll be fun! It's just a game, I promise. Besides, we've played before."

She walked to the window again. The sky was different than before, a creepy sort of darkness had crept its way in. It was a darkness that somehow seemed to make the shadows almost pitch but left the open areas untouched, a darkness that seemed unnatural, almost as if the sun was shining through some kind of colored filter. "I don't know, guys. I'm up for about anything, y'all know that. I don't really like this though. I just think that maybe we should—"

A strong gust of wind rattled the house, causing a series of shifts and pops all around them. Lightning streaked through the sky and another crash of thunder sent vibrations through the floor. One by one, large drops of rain blew in on the wind, colliding with the glass as if begging for their attention. It was coming, and it wouldn't be long before it was fully on them.

"Oh yeah," Scott said. "This is gonna be *good*. As long as..." he glanced at Rachel, eyebrows raised. "You're good to play. You know we gotta have ya."

Turning away from them, Rachel huddled next to the wall. She didn't *want* to do it. It was stupid. But she didn't want to tell them no and make them upset. She didn't want to admit to them that she was scared, and she *definitely* didn't want to admit to them, or to herself for that matter, that maybe she really did see something in the clouds earlier.

She didn't believe it. Not really. But she wasn't quite sure it was all made up, either.

Kris walked over and stood next to her, taking her shoulder and turning her around so they were eye to eye. "Come on, girl. It's just a stupid game, you know that. Just a way to pass the time. Besides, we *need* you to play. We gotta have four, remember? And I *want* you to play."

She scanned the room. Janet and Scott were both staring, hopeful looks in their eyes.

"How about it? We ain't got nothin' better to do. Storms gonna be too bad to go out for a while. Might as well see if we can make somethin' happen, right?"

"I just don't know. You know what they say about this kinda weather."

"I promise," Kris said, taking her hand. "Nothin' to be afraid of. You've played it before. We played a couple years ago at Aaron's party, remember? Nothing bad happened then." She looked to the window as a flash of lightening illuminated the night. "And nothing bad is gonna happen now."

Kris was right. They had played then, but this wasn't the same. There was no storm that night. But...nothing had happened. Rachel thought for a moment, then smiled, though it wasn't too convincing. "Okay. I'll play. I don't *want* to, but since the rest of you do, and you need four people, I'll do it. But just once."

"Fuck yeah!" Scott shouted. "I'll go grab some candles. Kris, can you get the matches from the second drawer, the one next to the fridge?"

"What can I do to help?" Janet asked, excited to finally have *something* to do.

Scott looked at her as he made his way across the house. "Just get ready to have some fun."

§

As they all sat down around a small circular table Scott used to play cards on with his friends, the wind began to pick up, stronger and more consistent, blowing from what seemed like every direction at the same time. With each gust they could hear the storm's breath howling at the seams of every window, almost as if it were prying at them with chilly little clawed October fingers, desperately trying to get inside. Rain was coming down in sheets, the sound of it pelting across Scott's roof every few seconds in massive waves drowning out nearly every other noise.

Scott struck a match and held it up to his face. The way the light darkened certain areas while accentuating others made him look creepy; the perfect look for what they were about to do. He lit four candles, placing one in front of each of them.

"Okay. So, how's this work? What's the name of this

game?"

He eyed them one by one for effect, then in a low, deep voice, he said, "the name of the game is Miss Molly, Miss Molly."

Janet pursed her lips, eyebrows furrowed. "Hmmm. Doesn't seem too scary to me. How do you play?"

"It's easy. You need four people in a circle, just like this. We all have to hold hands, close our eyes, and chant a phrase. Pretty simple. The candles have to stay lit, though, or it won't work."

"Oh," Janet said. "So, it's like Bloody Mary or something, is that it?"

"Kinda," Kris said, "but...kinda not."

Scott and Kris giggled. They were both giddy with excitement.

"Well, I've played Bloody Mary a bunch of times. We used to play it back in Cali when we were kids. Say her name three times in a mirror with the lights out and she's supposed to come for you, right?"

"That's how you play Bloody Mary, yeah...but you don't know nothin' bout ol' Molly Je—"

"Wait," Rachel said. She looked around the table, around the room, her eyes darting about, twitching like crazy.

"What is it, Rach? You see her already?" Scott laughed. "Hell, we ain't even started yet!"

"Be quiet, stupid," Kris replied, not wanting to make her friend feel any worse about her anxiety.

"I just don't know that we should...I mean, with this storm and all, well...what if—"

Almost as if on cue, lightning flashed and the lights in the house flickered off, then back on again, several times.

Rachel screamed, startled by the thunder. "That!" she yelled. "What if the power goes out or something? Jesus Christ, w-we shouldn't be doing this."

"Wow," Janet said. "What's gotten into you? This must be some story, huh?"

"You don't know about her. You're not from around here," Rachel said. "People take it seriously. Scott, please? We shouldn't be doing this and you fucking *know* it. You *know* what they say."

"It's okay, Rach. It's just a story, remember? Like I said earlier. It's just a game."

"Calm down, Rachel. Goddamn." Scott said, borderline scolding her. "As I was *tryin'* to say before I was so *rudely* interrupted, it's a game based on a story 'bout a little girl 'at used to live up the holler here. Her name was..." He paused, looked around as if expecting to be interrupted again. He eyed Janet, staring at her with intent, and whispered the name. "Molly Jenkins."

They all fell silent for a moment, each of them exchanging glances with one another as the name rang in the air like a rotten fruit refusing to fall from the tree. It was one Scott, Kris, and Rachel knew, one they'd heard many times before, even if only in hushed whispers. It wasn't a name discussed often in Pine Grove, especially in public, and it was typically only used as a warning to those who dared venture into the wrong places, or by drunk or high teens tempting fate by playing the very game they were about to play tonight.

Molly Jenkins.

It wasn't that they really thought anything bad would

happen, especially Scott or Kris, but they'd been conditioned with that name their entire lives, it was one that was as close to forbidden as you could get in their little piece of the world. Even the *thought* of saying it, the simple fact that Scott had uttered it out loud, was almost blasphemous. It didn't sound like anything out of the ordinary, yet...as it was spoken... goosebumps crept up each of their arms as a certain tension filled the room, a feeling that they'd started something there was no going back from.

Rachel swallowed hard, she immediately thought back to the color of the sky, the swirling clouds, the things she'd thought she'd seen in them earlier in the night.

Figures.

A particular figure, maybe?

The stories. She shook her head, her breath still, nerves on edge.

No, she thought. *We can't do this.*

§

"Ooooo," Janet mocked, eyes wide as she laughed. "*Molly Jenkins*! What's so special about her?" She looked around the table, but nobody else seemed to be picking up on her attempt at humor. "Geez. Y'all *are* serious, huh?"

Scott nodded toward the window, his expression changing to a more serious one. "Well, they's all kinds of stories 'round here, girl, but they ain't none of 'em like hers. You see, Molly was the youngest of four children...'at's why we need four to play, by the way...all of 'em used to live in a cabin way back up in the head of this here holler. All her siblings were girls, and they say 'at Molly was just a little *different* than the rest of 'em was."

"Different?"

"Yeah, you know, sort of...off in the head. She had some kinda disorder, I guess. Probably ADHD or somethin' like 'at, but way back then nobody know'd what 'at kinda shit was. They say she was just *different*. That she talked to people 'at nobody else could see, all the time jerkin' and twistin' in weird ways, almost like bugs was crawlin' under her skin and eatin' away at her brain. You know, just fuckin' weird. All her sisters used to make fun of her pretty bad, callin' her all kinds of names and just generally pickin' on her, takin' her stuff, laughin' and all 'at, especially the oldest. Boy, she didn't care too much for her from what they say, and you can figure how Molly didn't like it too much. She tried to stand her ground, but she was just too little, 'specially against all three of 'em."

"Aww, poor little thing."

"Yeah...*sure*! One day all four of 'em was out in the woods playin' around, gatherin' walnuts and such, when a big ol' storm blowed in outta nowhere. They say it was the worst storm Pine Grove had ever seen. Almost flooded the entire town 'at night, I reckon. Well, their parents took off lookin' for 'em, and 'bout halfway up the holler they heard a scream like nothin' none of 'em'd ever heard before." He gestured toward the window again. "They say everybody in the valley heard it, even over the hellacious storm that was goin' on. Some say it sounded like a mountain lion, others say it sounded like a woman. Some even said it sounded like some kinda monster, somthin' evil. Eventually, they ran up on the oldest girl. She was kneelin' on the ground in a puddle of mud, on her knees, cryin' her eyes out. They tried askin' her what was wrong and where her sisters were, but she couldn't stop cryin'. Her momma hit the ground with her, tryin' to calm her down and get her to tell 'em what happened, where they were, but she just kept on sayin' the same thing."

Janet was still, her full attention on the story. "What? What was she saying?"

He took in a deep breath, pausing for dramatic impact, then let it out slowly. "All she'd say was 'at *He* took 'em."

"He? Who's *He*?"

Rachel shivered, standing to walk around the room as she shook her hands. "I don't like this story. It creeps me the fuck out every time I hear it. Especially—"

A rumble of thunder caught her off guard.

Kris jumped. "Tell me about it! I ain't heard it told 'is good in a *long* time, and the weather is making it even better!"

Scott nodded slowly, his eyes settling on Janet's. "Nobody knows who it was. Some folks believe was Satan, but others reckon it was just a demon or warlock or somethin'. I don't know which one is more likely, but ain't none of 'em sounds too good to me."

"Wait...what happened to the other kids? Molly and her other two sisters, I mean."

A hard clap of thunder erupted, jarring the house. Rain was falling harder with each passing second, the lightning flashing in rapid bursts, almost nonstop.

Janet's focus shifted to the window. She swallowed hard, the wind blowing at near gale force into the house.

"'Round about midnight, right when the storm was at its peak, Mr. and Mrs. Jenkins heard their oldest daughter, the only one they'd found to that point, start screamin' from her room. She was hollerin', 'It's *Him*! It's *Him*!'. They took off to see what she was goin' on about, and when they opened the door to her room, Molly was standin' there over her sister, soaked plum to the bone, both of 'em covered in blood, and Molly was fuckin' eatin' her sisters insides. They say she was holdin' a different organ in each hand, goin' at her like a starved, ravenous savage. They screamed for her to stop, but when she turned around, the person they saw didn't look like Molly no more. Said her eyes was coal black and she was just grinnin' from ear to ear."

Janet's eyes widened. "Holy fucking shit. That *is* creepy."

"'Elp. Fuckin' *crazy* is what it is."

"What happened to her after that?"

"They say Molly jumped out the window and went off into the storm, cacklin' like some kinda animal or monster or somethin'. When they went out lookin' for her, they didn't find Molly, but they did find the other two girls on the ground below the window. At least they assumed it was them. They say they wasn't no meat left on 'em. Just a bunch of bones. Parents ended up buryin' the three daughters and leavin' town a few weeks later, and rightfully so. I'd imagine, 'specially back in them days, if somethin' like 'at happened, the whole town would shun you for witchcraft or some shit."

"And...Molly? I mean, how long could a little girl survive out in the wilderness like that all alone?"

Scott chuckled. "'At's the thing. A little girl, all alone, probably not too long, especially back then. But based on how 'at story goes, Molly was far from a little girl anymore. They say the storm brought somethin' with it 'at night, conjured up some kinda evil or somethin'. I told you; Molly was always said to be a little different, a little on the opposite side of normal.

Some say she made a pact with the devil 'at night, some say she was possessed. Regardless, folks 'round here ain't too fond of bad storms, especially the older ones. They say that whatever it was 'at came in on 'at storm liked Molly. That it saw somethin' *different* in her and took her back with it. And still, to this day, every now and then when we get a really bad one, they say 'at whatever evil it is comes on back, and they say it brings lil' Molly with it to take even more blood. They say if you look just right, you can see it in the sky, in the rain, smilin' down at ya."

"Damn. I like this story."

"What can I tell ya, girl? They's just somethin' in the storms around here, somethin' different, like whatever was in Molly. And that's where the game comes in."

He looked at each of them sitting around the table. "Everybody ready?"

Kris nodded. "Let's do it."

Janet smiled, excited to see what it was all about. "I'm ready."

Rachel seemed hesitant, but held her hands out none the less.

§

"Okay. Everybody hold hands. We gotta make a complete circle."

Each of them took the hand of the person next to them.

"The point of this whole thing is to evoke the spirit of either Molly or one of her sisters. Again, 'at's why we need four people...'cause they was four sisters. They say that if you can do that, you can find out what happened to her and who or what exactly it was in the storm 'at night."

"So, this is more like a séance, then? I see! Oh, this is gonna be creepy!" Janet shifted in her seat, ready to get the show on the road.

"Okay then. One at a time, we have to call her name. I'll go first, and y'all repeat after me. They's two phrases 'at we gotta say, and keep your eyes closed through it all. Got it?"

Everybody nodded. They'd all played before, with the exception of Janet, so they were familiar with the ritual.

"The phrases are 'Miss Molly, Miss Molly,' and 'What happened that night?'. And remember, keep your hands locked and keep the candles burnin'."

"Why?" Janet asked.

"Because," Kris said, an excited smile on her face. "If we break hands, they say she can possess one of us. Take us over."

"Just...don't let go, got it?" Rachel looked at Janet, dead serious.

Janet rolled her eyes. "It's just a game, but okay. I got it."

"Okay, I'll go first, then repeat after me from left to right." Scott took in a deep breath and closed his eyes. "Miss Molly, Miss Molly."

There was a brief pause, then Kris chuckled. "Miss Molly, Miss Molly."

Rachel shook her head again, her voice low and nervous. "Miss Molly, Miss Molly."

Janet didn't hesitate. "Miss Molly, Miss Molly."

A strong wind blew another sheet of rain into the house, causing them all to jerk suddenly. Kris laughed, followed by Janet.

"What happened that night?" Scott said.

"What happened that night?" Kris repeated.

Rachel cleared her throat and sighed. "What happened that night?"

Janet was jittery now, expecting someone to grab her or shout once she spoke the phrase, so she tried to mentally ready herself for the shock. "What happened that night?"

A monstrous explosion of thunder sent a shockwave through the house, shaking every picture on the walls. The electricity flickered off, the only light remaining being that of the candles as they burned. A strong wind rattled the door, almost as if someone were trying to knock it down.

Surprised, Janet jumped, letting go of both Scott's and Rachel's hands.

Before she even had time to react, before any of them could move, a cold sensation ran up the back of Rachel's neck, like fingertips dragging against her skin. There was a breath in her ear, icy and dark. Barely loud enough to hear, a voice whispered to her. "Let me show you."

The wind pushed harder, so much so the door gave way, bursting open. A sheet of rain covered the floor, soaking Rachel's back and extinguishing the candle's flames.

"Holy *fuck*!" Kris shouted, jumping up to close the door.

"Jesus, that was fucking nuts!" Janet yelled with a laugh. "Goddamn! Really had me goin' for a second!"

Scott was doubled over with laughter. "That was perfect timin'!"

It was dark inside the cabin now, no electricity, no candles, the storm raging hard outside.

"You okay, Rach?" Kris asked. "I can't see anything in here."

"Hang on, I'll get some flashlights," Scott said.

"Rach?" Kris said again. There was no response. "Rachel? You okay?" She reached for her phone and pressed a button to illuminate the screen. She shined it toward Rachel's seat, but she wasn't there. "Guys, where's..."

She heard a noise in the corner of the room, barely audible over the storm. She felt gooseflesh cover her arms as she realized what the sound was. It was giggling, almost like that of a child. "Uhm..." she started, "Rach? Is that..." She turned on her phone's flashlight and shined it toward the sound. In the corner, there was Rachel, or at least what used to be Rachel. She was hunkered down in a ball, staring up, directly at her, an unnaturally sinister grin stretched from ear to ear. Kris screamed, dropping her phone in the process.

"What?" Janet shouted, turning toward her friend. "What's wro...what the fuck is that?"

The way Kris's phone landed showed the scene perfectly.

Janet saw Kris lying on the floor, her legs and arms twitching frantically, like an epileptic does when they seize. But it was no seizure. On top of her was...something, someone... drenched to the bone. Whatever it was had its face buried inside Kris's neck, blood gushing onto the floor with every beat of her weakening heart. It looked up at her, stringy, wet hair draped to the sides, crimson liquid dripping from thin, pale lips. Its eyes were pitch black, haunting and emotionless, a deranged, fucked up smile searing into Janet's brain.

"Scott!" she cried, staggering back into the wall. "Scott, please, help!"

The thing that used to be Rachel let out a cackle as it cocked its head sideways and scurried across the floor like a cockroach.

"Help me, please!"

Scott came rushing back into the living room, flashlight in hand, and shined the beam at Janet. "What's wro...holy *fuck*! Wh-what *is* that thing?"

It glanced toward Scott, the beam directly in its eyes. It didn't seem phased by the light, letting out another deafening laugh. It shot toward him instead, blood and slobber dripping to the floor as if it were a rabid dog. He glanced at Janet, who was crying now, still pressed against the wall. He looked back to Rachel, or rather to the thing she'd become, as it closed the distance between them. He turned to run, making it as far as the opening to the kitchen, but there was no escaping.

Janet watched as it jumped, leaping through the air like a wild beast, hands latching onto Scott's shoulders, feet kicking into the backs of his legs to force him to the floor. The flashlight flew from his hand and slid across the ground, it and Kris's phone the only sources of light in the whole place.

Janet was still from shock, tears streaming down her face like a busted faucet. The beam wasn't directed at them this time, but she could see their movements in the shadows. A hand rose and came down, striking Scott, almost in slow motion, the sound of his clothes tearing as claws tore into them, the sound of his flesh being ripped from bone amplified by the adrenaline coursing through her body. Snarls and gulps as whatever the thing was consumed him, piece by piece, bite by bite, until the screaming stopped.

Janet placed a hand over her mouth, attempting to quiet herself. Her erratic breaths, the sounds of snot gurgling in her nose and throat, not helping to conceal her location, as if she'd ever been truly hidden. A rumble of thunder erupted overhead, catching her attention, and she looked toward the door. She knew it was her only chance. She had to run, had to try. Across the room, she heard Rachel giggling, the sound of claws clacking against the floor as she moved. She caught a glimpse of a shadow moving. It was only a matter of time until it came for her, too.

Janet let out a scream and bolted for the door. Rachel ran for her, nearly catching her ankle just as she opened the door and pulled it closed behind her. She could hear clawing from inside as Rachel scratched away, doing her best to get out. The doorknob jiggled, the door itself rattling as she did her best to hold it closed, but the rain had soaked it, making it impossible to get a solid grip. Her hand slipped, and she stumbled backward, her feet trying to find purchase on the steps but failing.

She hit the ground hard, water splashing up and over her face on impact. Her hands found her eyes, rubbing and wiping at the mud. She stood and saw Rachel on the edge of the porch, crouched down on all fours, still smiling. She stopped, afraid to move. What if it was like a cat or something? What if it was waiting on her to move so it could pounce? As the rain came down in a torrential downpour, Janet watched as Rachel's focus shifted from her to something in the sky.

Pushing herself to her feet, she slowly turned around to see what was happening. The lighting was strange; it was night, but hints of red and purple brightened it just enough for her to make something out in the darkness. There, in the sky in front of her, a figure began to take shape. It wasn't in the clouds, no. It was closer, almost close enough for her to reach out and touch. It was taking the shape of a person, as if the rain were falling over someone invisible and breaking their silhouette as they floated there in mid-air. She wiped her eyes again as she tried to make out what or who it was, squinting and squeezing them open and shut, trying to clear them of water.

She shook her head hard, one final attempt at gaining better focus, and opened her eyes for the final time. The figure in the rain was standing in front of her now, an odd face taking form. Inky blotches in the place of eyes and mouth, the areas in between streaking water as if it were made up of the storm itself. Its arms to the side, it made no attempt to reach for her. It just stood there, staring at her, staring through her. She looked into them for a brief moment, drawn in by something stronger than her own willpower. She wanted to look away, but she just couldn't. Her body and mind wouldn't allow it. For a brief moment, if she looked at it in just the right way, she thought she could see something in there, something moving around deep inside those hollow eyes.

Little girls, maybe?

No...

Her heart began to accelerate even faster than before, and the figure began to laugh. "Miss Molly, Miss Molly," it hissed. "What happened that night? Show this young lady, won't you?"

Behind her, Janet felt a searing pain pierce her neck as Molly laughed.

FECESNURA:
THE DEMON LORD OF SHIT

FRANKLIN SAT IN THE CORNER BOOTH OF THE MAIN Street Diner and stared into the distance. To most, he probably seemed like an idiot staring at nothing, a moron, in a sense. But Franklin wasn't *just* staring.

Not at nothing, anyway.

There was one thing across the room holding his attention, one thing in particular. It was the one thing in the entire world that could always keep his focus and make him forget about all the shitty things the day may have thrown his way, which, in his case, was quite a lot...and quite often.

This *thing*...the one that held his focus so intently...was, of course, a girl. What else would a puberty ridden teenage boy occupy his mind with? Especially one as horny as poor ol' Franklin Douglas.

Her name was Rose, and she didn't have to be doing anything special to make him all giddy and fluttery inside. In fact, just the mere sight of her serving an elderly couple across the room carried him off to another world; a world that he often struggled distinguishing from reality. When it came to Rose, some would say that Franklin was a bit of a daydreamer. She was so goddamn attractive, though. Jesus fucking Christ! She was small and petite, beautiful jade green eyes, she was tight in *all* the right places, and she had the sweetest little smile that Franklin had ever seen. Even the way her silky blond curls reflected the sun as it shined through the window made her look like an angel to him.

Goddamn she was cute. *Perfect* even, and that's pretty much all there was to say about Rose as far as Franklin was concerned.

Someday, Rose, he thought to himself, smiling the smile of most gooning teenage perverts. *Someday we'll be together. Someday I'll run my hands all over that soft, milky-white skin of yours as I bury my face between those sweet little ass chee—*

Before the thought could even be finalized, Rose looked up at him, her eyes squinted, the faint hint of a grin stretched across her ruby lips. She stared for a moment, almost as if she'd heard his thoughts, as if they'd somehow made some sort of cosmic mental connection, though unintentional on Franklin's behalf, and she could suddenly read his mind.

Holy fuck! Franklin thought, his eyes widening as Rose turned and started in his direction. His heart rate increased as he racked his brain to come up with a reason...a non-sexual and significantly less perverted one...for why he'd been staring and drooling over her. If, in fact, she *had* read his mind, there was no covering it up. It's hard to come up with excuses and justifiable reasons as to why one would want to bury their face between someone else's ass cheeks.

Fuck, fuck, fuck! Think, Franklin. Think of something to say. Why were you looking at her like that? What were you doing? Nothing stupid either. FUCK!

It was one of those instances where the whole thing happened in the course of a couple seconds, but it seemed to drag out over hours in his mind. The fear of confrontation, the nervousness he got from it all building up. But it was inevitable. She was coming straight for him, and her eyes were directly trained on his.

"Hey there, Franklin," she said, the sound of her voice almost sweet enough to melt him into a puddle. "You weren't lookin' *my* way, were you?" She stuck her bottom lip out in typical pouty fashion, her eyes staring into his deeply nearly hypnotizing him.

"Wha...uh...I-I mea—"

"Shh," she said, placing her index finger against his lips to shush him. "Those were some pretty dirty things goin' on in that brain of yours, hmm big boy?" She winked and blew a kiss. "I'd be lyin' if I said it didn't turn me on a little. Nothin' in the world like havin' your asshole eaten. Ain't that right, Frankie baby?"

His heart pounding so hard now it nearly beat a tattoo on his chest, Franklin froze as he stared in disbelief at what was happening. Rose was there, right in front of him, saying things he'd only dreamt about. Her finger was even touching his lips!

"Mmm," she moaned. "Just trust me when I tell you that I *love* the feeling of a tongue flicking across my asshole."

His eyes twitching from side to side, Franklin looked around, confused as fuck. He ran through various scenarios in his mind trying to try and make sense of it all. This couldn't be real. There was no fucking way it was. Maybe she was mistaking him for someone else. Someone that maybe looked similar. But if that were the case, why did she say his name? The odds of someone else with the same name that looked nearly identical to him living in the same town were very low, but that had to be what was happening. It *had* to be a mix-up. He knew he wasn't Rose's type. She was into muscular guys. The athletes. The *jocks*, as the general population tended to call them. Not the likes of little ol' Franklin. But it wasn't impossible. Stranger things *had* happened.

As Rose stood there looking down at him, he decided that there was only one way to find out for sure. A nervous grin crept across his acne ridden face, and he nodded hesitantly back at her. "Y...you talkin' to me?"

She raised an eyebrow and chuckled. "Why, who else would I be talkin' to? You're the only Franklin I know. I mean, you *were* lookin' at me, right? Those naughty little thoughts weren't for anyone else's ears to hear, were they?" she asked with a playful frown.

"Well...uh...I mean..."

"I know they were meant for me, silly." She sat down next to him and placed her hand on his thigh, squeezing it forcefully as if she were about to give him some sort of semi-erotic massage. "Oooh, what do we have here? Why, Frankie... is that a summer sausage in your pocket or are you just happy to see me?" She snickered at her own joke, sliding her hand further up his thigh. "Wow! Nice and thick, too." She licked her lips again, and winked. "Just how I like 'em."

A warmth rushed over Franklin that started in his groin and spread quickly into his stomach, eventually radiating throughout his entire body in massive pulses. He'd felt this sensation countless times before, but it was always when he was alone in his room, sock in hand, looking at pictures of her. He'd dreamt of something like this happening before, but he never thought in a million years that it actually would. Yet here he was, sitting in a booth in the Main Street Diner, and Rose was stroking his rock-hard cock through his khakis.

"Mmmmm, I never knew you had such a massive dick, Frankie baby. *Thick* and *hard*," she said in a sultry whisper. "God*damn*, baby." Scooting closer, she slid her tongue around his ear lobe, caressing it gently as she nibbled.

Franklin grunted and began thrusting his hips back and forth as his cock throbbed with pleasure. Rose looked at him and he could tell that she was enjoying it, too...almost as much as he was. Everything else around them seemed to disappear. The other servers, all the guests and patrons of the restaurant. Everything and everyone except Rose and him. All he could hear now was a static roar that seemed to get louder with each passing second, engulfing every other sound but Rose's sweet voice. The feeling was too much for Franklin to take. Her hand felt so good on his cock as she stroked it through his pants, up and down its entire length. The sweet scent of vanilla filled his nostrils as she continued leaning into him, whispering unimaginable thoughts into his ear.

"I-uh...you should probably s-stop, Rose. I-I me...uh... oh no!" He was thrusting his hips uncontrollably against her hand now, and his face flushed a deep, fever red. He grunted again, trying to fight it, but her voice, her scent, her gentle yet aggressive touch was just enough to send him over the edge. "Uh...I-I'm...I'm cumming, Rose!" he yelled out as he felt his cock exploded, pumping pulse after pulse of hot, thick, creamy jizz into his pants. "Aaaaaahhhhhhhh!"

His body fully relaxed as a result of what had just been the best and most intense orgasm of his young life, Franklin sat there in the booth with his eyes closed. After a few seconds, a realization suddenly began to dawn on him. Little by little, his ears began to pick up the background noise again. Not just him and Rose, but all the normal sounds of a diner. Music playing on the jukebox, the bell ringing as the door opened and closed. It all came creeping back. But there was one sound that seemed to cut through all the rest. One specific sound that stood out to Franklin above all the others. A sound that sent a shock deep into the core of his system.

It was the sound of laughter.

Loud, deafening, ear-piercing laughter echoed throughout the entire room.

A sudden surge of adrenaline pumped through Franklin's body as he began to realize what had just happened. He opened his eyes and saw Rose standing before him, holding a pitcher of tea. The look on her face was not a good one. It was one that signaled pure and absolute disgust.

"Jesus Christ!" she yelled to him. "I asked if you needed a refill. Not if you wanted to bone! Holy shit, Franklin. Keep it in your pants you pathetic little pervert!"

"Wha-huh?" Franklin looked around to see a fully occupied dining room. His legs started to quiver as his fight or flight response kicked in. "Oh no. This...this isn't real. It *can't* be!"

The entire room erupted with laughter.

"Shut up," he yelled back at them, embarrassed as he turned his attention to Rose. "Please, Rose. I...I'm really sorry. I...it's not what you think. I mean, I'm not a pervert, I promise." In an attempt to explain himself and save what little face he could, not that there was much he could save now, he stood from the booth and reached his hand out as if begging to her. "Rose, please. I—"

The look on her face as he extended his hand was a mix of utter horror and hilarity, and it didn't take long for everyone else in the restaurant to follow suit as they pointed at him and laughed.

"What?" he shouted. "Why are you all pointing at me?" He stood there surveying the room in confusion, finally realizing where everyone was pointing. All of their fingers were aimed down at his lower half. "Holy shit...please tell me this isn't happening." He looked down, and what he saw was nearly enough to stop his heart. The crotch of his khakis had stained a dark tan color. They were wet now, and it looked as if he'd pissed himself. But he knew it wasn't piss. He knew from the daydream, from the feel of a warm and slimy substance slipping down his leg, the tenderness of his still semi-bulging cock.

His heart accelerated and his breathing grew shallow and fast.

"Minute man!" one boy yelled out. "Look at Frankie the minute man!"

"Look everybody, it's good ol' Fappin' Franklin," another said, causing the crowd to laugh even louder.

Franklin didn't so much care about the rest of them. He was used to being laughed at and picked on. The worst part of the whole thing, the part that really *hurt* him, was that Rose was laughing, too, and she was laughing harder than anyone else. In this moment in time, it was like she was using him for nothing more than her own personal comic relief.

His beloved Rose.

"Geez, what a little perv!" she said. "I know I'm hot, but goddamn! Creaming your pants just because I asked if you wanted a refill? You really need to get laid, loser!"

"No, Rose. D...don't do this. Please. Not like this," he pleaded.

"Like you could ever have a piece of this!" she yelled back, reaching around to slap her own ass.

He felt his lower lip quiver and his hands started to shake as a single tear rolled down his cheek. All around him, they were laughing. An endless roast he'd not been invited to and never even intended to be a part of. He turned and ran toward the door, determined to get out of the diner and back to the safety of his own room as fast as possible. "Out of my way!" he cried, flailing his arms wildly. "Just leave me alo—"

The feeling hit him like a brick; a quick, sharp, forceful strike to his stomach. Gasping for breath, he looked to his side and saw Jimmy McCloud, Rose's current *thing*, sitting in a booth next to him.

"Aww. That hurt little buddy?"

"L-leave me—" He tried to speak, but he was nauseous now, his stomach rolling like a series of waves in a tsunami. "I'm gon-I'm gonna...throw—" In a violent spasm, his lunch spewed from the pit of his stomach, exiting his mouth with a force akin to being shot out of a cannon, and it landed all over Jimmy. Heave after heave, bits of cheese and pepperoni mixed with milk and bile made its way from Franklin's gut onto Jimmy's lap.

In a collective sigh, the entire restaurant went silent.

"Why, you little son-of-a bitch!" Jimmy yelled. He stood up, sending a cascade of chunky puke crashing to the floor. "I'll fuckin' kill you!" He punched Franklin in the face this time, unfortunately getting a mixture of blood and vomit on his hand. "That'll teach you to hurl on me you little motherfucker. Fucking disgusting little shit!"

Franklin spun around and hit the ground hard, causing the mess of vomit he'd just made in the floor to splash up. He groaned and tried to push himself to his feet, but his hands kept slipping on the lumpy concoction.

"Stay down there and lick it up off the floor!"

His face scrunched in both pain and disgust, Franklin let out a cry causing everyone to laugh and taunt him even more.

"I said, *lick* it," Jimmy commanded, forcing Franklin's head against the floor with his boot. "That's a good boy."

In his cries, the thick yellow and white mess lurched its way back into his mouth as he gasped for air. He gagged and blew it out as best he could, but it was no use.

"And let this be a lesson to ya. Leave Rose alone from now on. She's my piece, and she don't want nothin' to do with you, ya fuckin' little loser pervert." He snorted and hocked, swishing a huge ball of mucous around in his mouth. He took Franklin's hair in his fist and pulled his head back so that he could look him in the eyes. Then, with all the force he could muster, he let the loogie fly.

A deafening splat echoed in the room as a giant, bright green ball of snot slapped against Franklin's cheek.

"Next time, I'll be force feedin' ya my shit. And if ya think I'm jokin', just try me."

"Leave me alone!" he screamed, finally able to free himself and get to his feet. "You'll be sorry, Jimmy! You and Rose both! You'll see! You'll be sorry you ever laughed at me!" Slipping and sliding in the nasty mess, Franklin ran out the door leaving a trail of vomit-stained footprints behind.

§

Franklin scowled as he paced back and forth in his room. "Eat your shit, huh? We'll see about that, *Jimmy*. We'll just see how that works out for you. And Rose..." He opened a picture of her on his phone, one he'd taken nearly a year ago without her knowing. "How *could* you? Making a goddamn fool of me in front of *everyone* like that. I fucking loved you!" His eyes squinted, he shook his head in disgust, in heartbreak. "You've done it now, though. Nobody humiliates me like that and gets away with it. Your time will come, too. We could've been so happy together."

Out of nowhere, there was movement in his pants and a feeling of excitement radiated through his loins. A sinister grin stretched across his face as his dick continued to shift position, stiffening effortlessly. "What's that," he said, still staring at the picture of Rose. "You thought I was mad at you? Oh, Rose," he chuckled. "Sure, I may hate you now, but that doesn't change the fact that you're hotter than fuck. And, well, I'll still rub one out to you. More than one, actually."

He placed his hand on the crotch of his pants and started rubbing, but before he was able to really get into it, a crusty feeling on the fabric reminded him of the recent tragedy. "Goddamnit," he said, realizing what it was. He looked down to find the area was covered in dried semen from earlier. It had formed a flaky white patch when it dried. "Fucking asshole. I've gotta get them back somehow. Eat his shit. Yeah, right. Like he could actually make me do that. What a fucking prick. What I *should* do is—"

He paused mid statement, a thought coming to him. It wasn't just any thought, though...it was genius. The *perfect* thought. Perfect for this situation, and even more than perfect for the likes of Jimmy fucking McCloud. Franklin grinned, the edges of his mouth curling up like those of a cartoon villain. "That's it," he whispered, an almost sinful tone to his voice. "Why didn't I think of it sooner? It's the perfect revenge. Disgusting, vile, horrifyingly beautiful...in its own way, of course...and just goddamn perfect."

He hurried over to his laptop and opened the browser. He stared down at the screen, a hauntingly devilish look in his eyes as his fingers typed away at what seemed like superspeed. "Eat *your* shit, huh, Jimmy? Well, how about I do you one better?" He started laughing maniacally, a sound that ventured into the realm of what most would call psychopathy. It was so loud, so horrifyingly crazy sounding, that any normal person passing by would almost certainly think he was a few marbles short of a full set. "How about I make *you* eat *my* shit! How about that, fuckface?"

Franklin was right. This was a genius plan. Especially as far as revenge was concerned. Or at least he'd convinced himself that it was. Though, revenge can skew one's decision-making abilities significantly. It was still a good plan regardless, but it wasn't without fault. There was one specific problem that came to mind; a rather large one, in fact. Jimmy was a big guy. He was taller, stronger, and more athletic than Franklin in almost every way. So how was he going to make it happen? What was he supposed to do, force feed Jimmy a big ol' turd? There was no way in hell that would fly. No. If he was going to do this, if he was going to make Jimmy McCloud eat his shit, he was going to have to do it the smart way.

He typed in every food item he could think of that looked

anything remotely like feces, placing the word *shit* in front of it. He tried shit cookies, shit brownies, and even shit truffles, though he wasn't even sure what the hell a truffle was, but none of the results suited him. Sure, he found several pictures of random items that *looked* like shit, but he already knew they looked like it. He needed recipes. He needed to know how to make these items while mixing his own bodily waste into them. He even tried the phrase *how to make an asshole eat shit*, but that one brought up results that no person should ever see. As it turns out, the internet is full of all sorts of... fetishes...if you will. Fetishes that, even considering all the things he'd imagined doing with Rose, made him gag.

As he scrolled through the various images of chocolate-based items that happened to resemble poop, a thought occurred to him. It came from something he'd seen in a movie a few years ago, something very similar to what he was trying to accomplish now. In the movie, a housekeeper had grown tired of dealing with her employers assholishness, so she decided to quit, but not before baking a chocolate cake with her own shit in it.

"Yes," Franklin whispered. "That's it! I'm going about this all wrong. I don't have to find a recipe specifically for *shit* food. I just need a recipe for something that *looks* like shit." That option seemed very doable, and significantly easier. He could just learn how to make cookies or brownies or something similar, something easy, and load it up with his own stinky ass cream. So long as the item was chocolaty and brown, the color of shit should blend in well and go unnoticed...until it was consumed.

In the browser, he changed the focus to extra chocolatey

foods. "Yeah...that'll do just fine," he said, clicking on a recipe for double chocolate fudge brownies. It was a basic recipe, one that even Franklin, a less than stellar baker at best, should be able to follow with relative ease. His grin stretching from ear to ear, he moved the pointer to the print icon and lifted his finger, but just before he clicked the mouse, he noticed something else on the screen. Something that wasn't part of the background. Something that wasn't supposed to be there.

"What...is that?" he leaned closer to the screen to get a better look. His eyes squinted, he concentrated on the image as it slowly came into focus. "What the fuck?" he whispered. He stood there, silent, motionless. A good many seconds passed as he tried to make sense of what he was looking at.

Then it moved.

Franklin's eyes grew wide as he realized he was staring at a reflection. There was someone, or *something*, standing in the room behind him.

"Why, hello there, Franklin," a wicked voice hissed. "I see you want to get *even*, hmm?" The thing moved again, causing Franklin to jump.

"What the fuck!" he yelled, drawing out the last word as chill bumps crept over the length of his arms. He spun around in the chair to face the intruder; hands balled into fists as he readied to defend himself. "Who the fuck ar—holy shit!" he gasped, laying eyes on the intruder for the first time. "Wh-wh-what the fu-fu-fuck?" His knuckles turned white as he gripped the chair's armrests tightly, his feet looking for purchase as he scooted back into his desk. He didn't know what it was, but he knew for damn sure that it wasn't a person.

A dirty, skid-mark brown in color, it floated above him,

hovering like some sort of dirt covered fairy. Its skin was lumpy and rough looking, though it seemed to shine in a stomach-churning way as the slightest hint of light caressed its strangely textured, yet smooth, surface. Its body took no standard shape, aside from being awkwardly long and thick. Its legs and arms were short, too, its head the most human-like appendage about it.

"I saw what happened to you today," it hissed. "What a horrible thing that boy did. How embarrassed you must have been...must *still* be."

Franklin sprang from the chair and stumbled toward the door. His head jerked from side to side, his brain unsure of what was happening. "What the fuck are you? How did you get into my room?"

It smiled at him, revealing rows of little brown nuggets, jagged and worn, in the place of what should have been teeth. "Where do you think you're going? I'm here to help you, Franklin. Don't you wanna get back at them? Come on, it'll be fun. How 'bout it?" It chuckled, forcing a series of loud, flatulent spurts from its asshole. With each fart, the stench of sulfur and methane grew stronger until it nearly overpowered Franklin.

"What is that *smell*! Goddamn! Make it stop! God, please, make that smell go away!"

The thing looked at Franklin as if offended, but it was more out of annoyance than embarrassment. "Apologies, *boy*. An unfortunate side effect of my rank in the demonic realm. Let me introduce myself. My name, is Fecesnura. I am the demon lord of *feces;* the master of *shit*." Gliding through the air, it came closer to Franklin, offering its hand for him to shake.

"Demon of *feces*? You mean..." Franklin yanked his hand back. Something about the thought of shaking hands with a literal shit demon was a bit unsettling. "But you don't really *look* like a demon. I mean...I thought demons looked, well... different. They're always seducing sexy women in the movies, and they're always rich and powerful. Either that, or they look like little red men with pitchfork tails. Pardon me for saying so, but you don't look rich *or* powerful. You look like, well...a piece of shit."

Fecesnura hung his head. "Yeah. That's kind of a long story. Suffice it to say, I was a bad little *shit*." He raised his head and stared, eyes burning like coals of fire. "Pun intended. But I digress. Let's get back to business. That's the whole reason I'm here, after all. Business. Do you want to get even with Jimmy, or not?"

"What kind of a question is that? Of course I wanna get even. That's what I was doing before you showed up. Coming up with a plan to do just that. A *brilliant* plan, too, if I do say so myself."

"Yes, I know what you were doing. I was watching you. You want him to eat shit, if I'm not mistaken. *Your* shit, to be exact."

"Yeah. That was the plan. Why? Something wrong with it?"

Fecesnura grinned, his fiery eyes narrowing to tiny little slits. "No. Not at all. It's a beautiful plan, in fact."

"I thought so," Franklin said, a bit of arrogance in his response.

"I can give you that power, if it's what you desire. I can give you the power to make it happen. All you have to do is say *yes*."

Franklin paused, cocked his head to the side. "Wait a minute. If you're a demon, and you're offering me help, aren't you supposed to be trying to steal my soul or something? I mean, you have to want something in return to help me, right? That's how it always is in the movies and stories and such."

"Ha! I'm the lord of *shit*! My freedoms are very minimal. Daddy rarely lets me do anything fun. I have to find *something* to keep me occupied throughout all eternity. This makes for a good distraction. Regarding payment, I wouldn't worry too much. It *is* souls that I feed on, but I'm not particularly interested in yours. Rotten souls for a rotten demon. That's how it works. The soul of the boy who mocked you will be much better than yours. Much more sour, more vile. We have *rules*, you know. Even in Hell."

"Rules? But I thought that—"

"Do you want my help or not?"

"Well, I mean—"

"I'll warn you now, though, because it's required. Once you agree, there's no backing out. If you do, it'll be your soul that accompanies me back home, and neither of us want that. I love souls, but yours is not *rotten* enough. Not *yet*, anyway."

Franklin stood there for a moment thinking about the offer. Dealing with a demon was something he'd never really thought about. Hell, until now, he wasn't even sure he believed in such things. But now, here in front of him, was a real life, honest to God demon, offering his services. Why not take all the help he could get? Arching his back and jutting out his chest in a sense of dominance, Franklin grinned. "You know what? I don't have anything to lose. The whole school just watched me cream my fucking pants to a goddamn daydream. Rose hates me. She made it perfectly clear that I'm nothing more than a joke to her. Jimmy is probably gonna beat the shit out of me again on Monday, too, and who knows how many more times after that, just because he can. Why the hell not? Yes, I could use some help getting back at him. Sure!"

Fecesnura's glowing eyes grew wide, an uncomfortably eerie heat radiating from them. "We have a deal then?"

"I said yes, didn't I?"

Holding up his stubby little arm, Fecesnura produced a worn slip of paper, ragged and stained a dull piss colored yellow. "Follow these instructions exactly as they appear. If you do, then your revenge will be had."

"Don't I have to sign a contract or something? We are making a deal, right?"

"Again, you watch too many movies, boy." He floated higher until he reached the ceiling, and smiled down at Franklin. "We have a verbal agreement. That's legal and binding in Hell. As long as you follow through with the instructions, our dealings are done and your soul will remain *yours*. Back out, and, well...things won't be good for you."

"Hmmm. Okay, I guess a verbal contract is good enough. Don't worry, I fucking *hate* Jimmy McCloud. I'd never dream of backing out of this."

"It's been a pleasure, Mr. Franklin. I'll be watching." Fecesnura opened his mouth and a powerful stream of chocolate brown sludge spilled over Franklin, covering him from head to toe.

"Jesus, man! What was that for! You're fucking sick. This smells like *shit*!" He wiped his eyes as best he could, then looked up. Fecesnura was gone. "Great! Leave me another fucking mess to clean up, too."

A demonic laugh echoed in the air. "I told you, I have to find *something* to keep myself occupied."

§

On the paper was a list of four items, each very specific in nature. Franklin was to collect and mix them together, then consume them before the stroke of midnight. The thought of sweet revenge on Jimmy McCloud, the boy who'd humiliated him in front of everyone, in front of his beloved *Rose*, was too good to pass up. Besides, according to the demon, he had to try now; otherwise, his soul would be doomed to an eternity in *shit* Hell with ol' Fecesnura, and he wasn't sure he could stomach the smell.

First, it called for something from Franklin's body. This was supposed to bind him to the deed. It was a way to link the revenge to him specifically so that a minimal number of civilian casualties were had. Examples of acceptable items included hair, skin, blood, or other bodily fluid. He decided that a small snip of his own hair would be the easiest to get, so he clipped a chunk from the back of his head and tossed it into a paper cup.

Next, it called for food. Something heavy and dense, preferably high in fiber. This would help *solidify* things and add to the discomfort of the victim. The spicier the food, the worse the victim suffered, and this was something Franklin thoroughly enjoyed the thought of. He went downstairs and opened the refrigerator. He'd remembered having a somewhat spicey dinner a couple nights ago, and there had to be some leftovers in there somewhere. As he opened each drawer, he scanned the contents, finally finding a log of habanero and jalapeno infused sausage.

"Not the spiciest, but I guess it'll do."

Third, the list called for a laxative. Franklin went to the medicine cabinet and grabbed what was left the Milk of Magnesia his dad had used last month when he'd had a bad case of hemorrhoids. His dad had never been one to take many medicines, but he'd complained about the discomfort so much that his mom made him take it. This ingredient, the list said, was to move things along. It had worked for his dad...so it made sense.

As Franklin poured the Milk of Magnesia into the cup with the hair and sausage, he read the final item on the list.

"What the hell?"

It called for something from the body of the victim. "How am I supposed to get that?" He paused, then remembered something in the waste basket beside his bed. "Hmmm." He read over the list again, double checking acceptable options. "More body fluid, huh?"

He ran back to his room and rummaged around in the trash, pulling a chunk of wadded up tissue from its depths. "I can't believe I'm doing this." Slowly, he unfolded the cold, wet clump of tissue revealing a sticky green slime. It was the tissue he'd used to wipe the remains of Jimmy's snot wad from his face. "Well, this *is his* body fluid," he said, tearing off a thumbnail sized piece and tossing it into the milky white liquid. "Now, to blend!"

He ran downstairs and grabbed the blender. He added a bit of water to assure there was enough liquid to blend, and tossed the contents of the cup in. The addition of the sausage made for a thick, lumpy mess, but surprisingly, the booger coated napkin seemed to blend well into with the rest. "Great," Franklin said, holding the concoction up in front of him. "This'll feel really good on my tongue. What did I get myself into?"

Holding his nose, he poured the contents into a glass, put it up to his lips, and chugged.

"Now I have to...wait...*what*?"

Franklin read the final task on the list, and he wasn't quite sure that it wouldn't lead to him getting several broken bones. Especially if Jimmy caught him.

"What the fuck," he said, his stomach beginning to growl in opposition. "I gotta get moving."

§

It worked fast.

Within fifteen minutes of downing the nasty sausage and booger juice, Franklin found himself squeezing his ass cheeks as he struggled toward Jimmy's house. It was the worst case of the walking shits he'd ever had. With every step the farts seemed to last longer, to get louder and wetter until the familiar feeling of swamp ass consumed him.

"Th-th-this is-uuugggghhhhhh!" Another fart burst from his asshole, sending a stream of liquid into his boxers. "Fuck me!" he screamed. "I'll never ma-make i-eeeewwwwww!" Another fart, another stream of liquid, every toot feeling more and more like a sprinkler shooting out of his colon.

He rounded the corner at Maple and Oak, and there it was, Jimmy's house, shining in the night like a lighthouse beacon in a raging storm. "Fuck yeah! Longest quarter mile I've ever wal-ke-d. Oh fuck!" The stain on his ass grew larger as his brown-eyed poo faucet continued to spew mist. "Jesus! On-ly a f-ew more ste-p-s!"

In a wild leap, Franklin thrust himself up the steps and against the door. He dropped his pants and doubled over, a slur of loud grunts and moans spilling from his mouth as he released a spicy mist of chocolate-colored sewage. "Fuck! Yeeeeaaaaaahhhhh!" With each grunt, air exited his shitter with a force rivaling that of a hurricane. "Goddammmmmnnnnnn!"

Squatted down and facing the street, Franklin heard the front door open behind him.

"What the fuck?" a strong voice protested.

Too deep into the orgasmic pleasure of emptying his bowels to care, the scenario didn't register with Franklin right away. "Ahhhh yeahhhh!" he moaned, as his flatulence continued to splatter mist all over the front porch.

"Franklin?" Jimmy looked down at him in disbelief.

Franklin was still mid-squat directly in front of him, a steady stream of ass juice flowing at his feet.

"What the fuck is going on?" He scanned the porch, now nothing more than a thick layer of brown sludge. "Are you... are you *shitting* on my porch? I'm gonna fuckin' kill you!"

Franklin continued to push, the force distending his rectum, puckering from his ass like a set of thick and juicy mud-covered lips. "Here it comes!" Like giving birth to a twelve-pound child, he pushed one final time. A turd the size of a football ejected from his now swollen and bleeding asshole, sending splashes of the mess up onto Jimmy's legs.

"Holy shit! That's fucking disgusting!" Jimmy yelled.

Finally able to concentrate on something other than his ass contractions, Franklin turned around, sweat dripping from his forehead, his eyes drooping in an exhausted and worn gaze. With tired breath, he looked at Jimmy and recited the line exactly as Fecesnura had written. "Eat my shit, Jimmy McCloud, and lick its crumbs from your lips."

"Oh, you're a dead man walkin', buddy."

Franklin's eyes widened and he stumbled backward, slipping in his own poopy slime. "B...but you're supposed to eat it! That's all the note said to do! I did everything right! Exactly as he wrote it!"

Jimmy moved out onto the porch, navigating around the nastiness as best he could. "Is that right?" He bent over and grasped Franklin's collar, pulling him up to a standing position. "I told you what would happen. Remember?"

Franklin squinted, bracing himself for the worst. "But it was supposed to work!"

Jimmy drew his fist back, zeroing in on Franklin's face, but before he could unload, a noise from behind them drew their attention. It was a gulping sound, like someone drowning in the shitty pool or choking on the partial chunks left in it. Curious, he threw Franklin to the ground and spun around. "Goddamn, son! What did you shit out?"

The massive turd was moving. It wiggled around at first, from side to side like a snake. The gurgling sound grew stronger, bubbles forming in the liquid around one of its edges. The thing began to shake violently as if seizing, until large chunks of partially digested material ripped from each of its sides to take shape as legs and arms.

Both boys stood, staring at the unbelievably large shit log rolling and thrashing around in the lake of poo.

"Is it *alive?*" Jimmy muttered.

Franklin was quiet and motionless beside him. He had no idea what was happening either.

Jimmy elbowed his nemesis. "Hey, I asked you a question fuckface. What the fuck is that thing?"

"I...I'm not really sure."

In one smooth action, the turd rolled completely over and rose to a seated position. It had eyes and a mouth carved into its brown, lumpy face, and it raised one arm and pointed at Jimmy. "Eat his *shit*," it hissed. Although there were no fingers, its stubs were tipped in long polished and pointed claws. Uneven chunks of randomly placed hair covered its head.

"Holy Hell. It's *my* hair." Franklin said. The realization shocked him. He knew what the thing was now. It was a demon, summoned from the depths of Hell to exact *his* revenge. It wasn't there for him. It was there for Jimmy.

It jumped to its feet and lunged at the bully, forcing its way into his mouth.

"Fu-ck! H-hel—" Jimmy muttered, chocking on the large animated turd. Grasping his throat, he staggered around as he tried to fight the beast, only to slip on the assbile-soaked floor. As he lay there, he looked to Franklin, desperation in his eyes.

The thing worked its way into his throat and down his esophagus. His neck bulged and stretched with each inch the demon gained. From his chest cavity, one of its claws protruded, slicing him open down to his groin. Blood and organs spilled over the porch in a great wave, like something out of an old B-rated horror movie. It mixed with the liquid shit, rushing over Franklin's feet and covering his shoes.

The demon turd leaped from Jimmy's now lifeless body,

grinned at Franklin, took a bow, and fell apart into the bodily fluids from which it came.

Speechless, Franklin fell to his ass. He was trembling, partially from disbelief and partially because he knew that he was now responsible for a murder. Maybe not directly, but he'd most definitely been at least a partial cause. His DNA was everywhere. The police would certainly come looking for him. What would he say? Technically, *he* hadn't killed anyone. But how would he explain it?

"What am I supposed to—"

"Don't worry," a familiar voice said. "I'll take care of it...for the right price, that is."

He looked up and saw Fecesnura hovering in the air above him. "What do you mean?" Franklin said. "How will you do that?"

"Would you like to make another deal?"

"What? Another...what *kind* of deal?"

Fecesnura floated closer to the boy. "A very *good* deal. You give me another soul, and I'll clean the evidence away. All ties to you will be forgotten. It'll be as if they'd never existed."

"Another soul? Not *my* soul!"

"No," Fecesnura replied. "I need another *rotten* soul, remember?"

"Who?"

The corners of Fecesnura's lips curled into an evil grin. "Rossssse," he hissed. "Feed her to me and you'll be free."

Franklin sat there, studying the little demon, the situation as a whole. He knew if he did nothing, he'd be done. He'd spend the rest of his life in jail, followed by an eternity with his new friend, vomiting endlessly from his disgusting stench.

"But, I can't. Not Rose."

"Then I guess I'll have to settle for you. Not my preference, but in tough times one takes what one can get."

"Wait," Franklin said. "If I take you to Rose, what happens then? Will I be linked to that murder?"

"Oh, I'm sure by then we will be able to make one *final* deal. One to clean everything up quite nicely."

Somewhere deep down, Franklin still had feelings for Rose, but he couldn't go out like this. And besides, she was part of the whole damn thing; part of the whole reason he'd gotten into this mess in the first place. "Fuck," Franklin said. "I guess you leave me with no choice. Sure. What's one more, right?"

"Exactly," Fecesnura laughed, "what's *one* more?"

ABOUT THE AUTHOR

Tony is the author of *Folktale, Sour, Wicked Appalachia, The 11th Plague*, and *A Bad Case of Tinnitus*. He has also authored over two-dozen short stories that have appeared in various print and online horror and dark fantasy magazines and anthologies. Tony was born and raised in the Appalachian foothills of eastern Kentucky (he currently lives in southern Indiana) and his fiction is largely influenced by the folktales and legends he grew up listening to. Tony's ability to retell and put his own spin on those old folktales while keeping their Appalachian roots intact is what sets him apart from others in the field, and his story telling is unmatched.

For a glimpse into his daily life and to stay up to date on all his fiction, including current and upcoming releases, as well as his latest horror projects, follow Tony @tonyevanshorror, or visit tonyevanshorror.com.